As a demon under the Horseman of Famine, Beltine enjoyed helping his horseman take out a coven of witches. It was a wonderful change of pace—doing something other than spreading famine upon different areas of the human plane. When Famine teams up with his brothers to track down a dangerous and mysterious artifact, Beltine is happy—and honored—to be chosen to help. Their information takes them to an exotic animal rescue facility in the mountains of Idaho. Upon getting there, they discover that some of the animals aren't animals—they're shifters trapped in animal form. What really shocks Beltine is that one of the males is his *amina*—his soul. Except, Beltine is still a couple of decades away from his thousandth birthday. Still, once his *amina*—Kavan—finally returns to his human form, Beltine finds himself just like any other paranormal. He wants what the Moirai have deemed his. With his time in service to Famine not yet up, as well as trouble still on the horizon, Beltine isn't certain what his best move is. Will even the help of his horseman be enough to find an answer?

The Early Amina
Copyright © 2021 Charlie Richards
ISBN: 978-1-4874-3391-8
Cover art by Angela Waters

Published by eXtasy Books Inc

Look for us online at:
www.eXtasybooks.com

The Early Amina
A Loving Nip Book 26

By

Charlie Richards

DEDICATION

Strength doesn't come from what you can do. It comes from over-coming the things you once thought you couldn't.
~Unknown

Chapter One

"Beltine, Master Famine is looking for you."

Turning, Beltine spotted Garnelle. He nodded respectfully at the slightly older demon and replied, "Thank you, Garnelle. Do you know if he's in his office?"

Garnelle smiled, surprising Beltine. The demon was a decade older than Beltine's own nine-hundred-seventy-eight years, and he wasn't known for his warm and fuzzies. In fact, Beltine couldn't actually remember the last time he'd seen a true, relaxed smile on Garnelle's face.

"No," Garnelle replied, amusement lacing his tone. "Famine and his men are relaxing in the bathing chamber."

Beltine cocked his head, furrowing his brows. "The bathing chamber?"

Knowing the room to which Garnelle referred, Beltine wondered at that. Each Horseman of the Apocalypse ruled their section of the demon realm. Famine had originally designed it in what many would consider a Roman style, with communal cathedral baths. A couple of centuries before, Famine had changed their home to a style more along the line of an Arabic sheik's palace, but everyone had loved the communal baths so much that, after a little redesign, Famine had kept it.

The corners of his lips twitching, Garnelle told him, "Hank calls it a swimming pool."

Blinking, Beltine processed that. Master Famine had bonded with three men only a week before. Hank was a sweet and friendly human. His second lover—the vampire,

Chissom—had a fun-loving and laid-back attitude with a dash of mischievousness added in. Famine's third lover—a red fox shifter named Knossis—had a dominant and forceful personality and still kept his position of head enforcer for his skulk.

"Hank thinks it's a swimming pool, and Master Famine didn't explain that the demons use it to . . . bathe?" Beltine felt his way around that question slowly and realized the answer as soon as he finished it. "Because Master didn't want to embarrass his lover."

Garnelle nodded once. "Probably." With a smirk and a wink, he advised, "Everyone is being advised to keep a bathing suit handy . . . just in case."

Unable to help himself, Beltine groaned. "But bathing naked is the point."

Shrugging, Garnelle pointed out, "You're only a couple of decades away from finding an *amina*. Once that happens, you won't want him or her to be naked in front of another." Garnelle's expression sobered. "And that person won't want your willie dangling for all to see, so it can't hurt for you to get used to not being naked in front of others."

Beltine recognized the wisdom in that and nodded. "You, too." Resting his hands on his hips, he clarified, "You're a decade older than me, aren't you?"

"I am." Garnelle's expression turned wistful. "Another twelve years." Sobering, he cleared his throat. "Not that I'm counting down or anything."

Scoffing, Beltine muttered, "Of course not. None of us are." Then he started toward the door. "Thank you for the heads up."

Garnelle replied, "You're welcome," before exiting the library in another direction.

Beltine strode swiftly through the massive palace. While the library was on the main floor, it was on the opposite side as the bathing chambers. That was to keep the possibility of moisture damage away from the books.

He made his way to the room that housed half a dozen pools, each having a different temperature. They ranged from cool and inviting, good for swimming, to hot and soothing, excellent to help sore muscles. He'd enjoyed them all many times over his long life.

Spotting Chissom exit a corridor to the left and turn in the same direction, Beltine took in his attire. The vampire was dressed in a pair of board shorts and flip-flops. He carried a towel draped over his shoulder.

Making a split decision, Beltine called to Chissom as he picked up his pace.

The vampire paused, half-turning. His kind hazel eyes crinkled at the corners as he smiled at Beltine. "Hey, man." Cocking his head, he asked, "Uh, sorry. There's a lot of you to remember. Who are you again?"

Beltine wasn't offended. After all, Famine had over two hundred demons under his command. There were only a few generals — those demons who'd served a thousand years and had been blessed by the gods with their *amina* — their soul. The rest of Famine's demons were of various ages, from a few years old to almost a thousand. As Chissom had said, there were definitely a lot of them.

"I'm Beltine," he told Chissom. "And I totally understand." Falling into step beside the vampire, he hesitated a second before saying, "I heard that Hank thinks the bathing chamber is a swimming pool."

"Bathing chamber," Chissom repeated, his eyes narrowing just a little. Just as quickly, they widened. "Oh, *bathing* chamber. Shit!"

Holding up his hands, palms out, Beltine hurried to add, "We've all been warned to have shorts handy, but I didn't want Hank to find out his mistake in some . . . unkind way."

Chissom nodded slowly, his expression one of thoughtfulness. "So you decided to come to me."

Beltine admitted, "I spotted you on your way there, and the idea just sort of . . . popped into my head." Grimacing, he told him, "If I had to guess, Master Famine would probably order us all not to say a word about it."

After grunting softly, Chissom mused, "But that leaves it open for someone to say the wrong thing at the wrong time or for Hank to overhear some random comment." He shook his head. "Then he might jump to a wrong conclusion, like thinking we were lying to him."

Grimacing, Beltine stated, "I hadn't even thought of that. I just didn't want to see him accidentally hurt."

"I appreciate it, Beltine," Chissom replied, reaching up and patting his shoulder. "I'll deal with it."

Beltine nodded. While he hated landing a problem at Chissom's feet, he wanted to help, too. His master deserved happiness, but he didn't have any relationship experience. While Beltine didn't actually have any, either, he'd spent so much time in the human realm that he'd seen examples of what to do as well as what not to do.

Keeping secrets — even when good intentioned — definitely fell into the *not to do* category.

"I'm surprised you're out here," Beltine commented. "I would have thought you'd already be in with Famine and Hank. I heard they were there."

When Garnelle had told him that Famine and his men were in the bathing chamber, he'd assumed it included all of them.

"I was just finishing up talking with Master Dante," Chissom explained, referring to the vampire master of his coven. Dante Mannis had been supplied with a bespelled mirror, allowing him to communicate with those in the demon realm, as electronic devices didn't work there. "Some of our people were tracking down an address we needed."

Beltine nodded, figuring he knew what that had to have been about. The whole reason Famine ended up involved with Chissom, Hank, and Knossis was indirectly due to a circle of witches. Famine and his brothers had originally thought they'd wiped out that particular circle, but one of the leaders must have escaped and rebuilt it. They'd ended up more dangerous than ever, using blood magick to screw up the hands of The Fates. The Horsemen were working with the vampires to figure out possible hiding places for The Red Book — a tome of ancient and dangerous spells.

Just where did the damn thing come from, and how did these witches stumble across it?

Beltine figured he would hear those answers eventually, but he guessed Famine wanted to see him to give him a new assignment.

Or I'll be assigned to monitor the activities of a younger demon.

Due to the dangers the circle of witches had caused, and not knowing who else might have access to The Red Book — the brothers didn't plan to make the same assumption twice — any demons under five hundred years were being escorted by an older one. The Horsemen had each lost several demons before instituting the safety precaution. Somehow, the witches had figured out how to track where a demon would appear on the human plane and trap them, allowing them to use demon blood for their magick.

It was really fucking with The Fates. The Moirai had even inadvertently lined up Knossis to be mated with someone unsuitable. Fortunately, when Knossis had bonded with Famine, that tie had been broken, allowing the shifter to find happiness with the other men.

Spotting the large, gilded, double-doors, Beltine hurried a few steps to reach them first. He gripped the right one and pulled it open. With the weight of the door, he wondered how Hank managed to move them.

Beltine knew that newly created demons struggled for the

first few years of their life until they'd toned up a bit.

Then Beltine realized there was probably always someone around the cute, plump human to do that sort of thing for him.

"Thank, Beltine," Chissom said with a grin, showing off his fangs. "But you really didn't need to escort me."

Moving inside, Beltine told him, "I was told Master Famine needed me, so it was my pleasure."

"Oh, yeah?" Chissom swept his gaze around the massive chambers. Once he spotted his lovers, he started in that direction. "Wonder if it has anything to do with the address Master Dante gave me."

Beltine released the door and once again fell into step beside Chissom. "I look forward to learning."

Sweeping his gaze over Master Famine — who reclined in a pool on a carved reclining seat with Hank sitting on his lap — Beltine appreciated the relaxed expression on his face. His master had been so stern and stoic for centuries. Since bonding with his three men, he was learning to smile more often.

It was fantastic to see.

"Ah, Chissom," Master Famine purred, lifting his hand and beckoning. "So glad you joined us."

Chissom placed his towel on a nearby recliner, kicking off his flip-flops. Then he did as Famine asked and joined his lovers in the pool. Stopping beside the pair, Chissom delivered a slow, sensual-looking kiss to both Famine and Hank. By the time the vampire was finished, Knossis had arrived, pausing in the laps he'd been swimming. Chissom offered the big shifter the same sultry lip-lock.

Beltine found it fascinating that all the men smiled and watched as they kissed each other, not a hint of jealousy in sight. While he'd never had a relationship, he wondered how that worked. He supposed that, as long as it never changed, it really didn't matter.

After Famine finished kissing Hank and Knossis, too, he turned his attention to Beltine. "Thank you for coming, Beltine."

Dipping his head in deference, Beltine replied, "Of course, Master Famine. I live to serve you."

The corners of Famine's lips twitched as he nodded. "We have several leads as to where the witch circle could be hiding the book," his horseman stated. "My brothers and I are each taking a place to search. Our location is in Idaho. I would like you to put together a squadron of demons. Three teams of five. You will lead them."

Beltine's jaw sagged open. For an instant, he just stared, hardly believing what he'd just heard. He wasn't a general, but Master Famine was giving him the duties of one.

"Oh, you just shocked the shit out of him, Famine," Hank murmured, sounding amused. "Remember to keep breathing, Beltine."

Hearing Hank's words, Beltine pulled himself together. He snapped his mouth shut and bowed low, keeping his wings tight against his back. After a second, Beltine felt Famine's slender fingertips touch his temple, so he straightened.

"I am truly honored by your orders, Master Famine," Beltine stated, his comment heartfelt. "When do we leave?"

Famine turned his attention to Chissom, who had settled beside Hank in the water. "Has your coven given you an address?"

Chissom nodded. "Yep. He'll have a dossier waiting for us to pick up within the hour."

Smiling a bit, Famine hummed. "Excellent." He turned his attention back to Beltine. "You have two hours. Assemble in the courtyard." Then Famine narrowed his eyes and pinned a hungry look on Knossis. "I've enjoyed watching your large muscles move beneath your skin while you swam, Knoss. I believe we have time for me to explore them."

Realizing he'd been dismissed, Beltine backed up a step. When Famine moved Hank to Chissom's lap and lunged at his huge shifter lover, Beltine turned and headed out of the bathing chambers. He paused at the door just long enough to hit a button, which illuminated a red light to the right of every entrance.

It was a newly installed device, warning every demon not to enter.

Beltine hurried through the halls, ticking off names in his head and wondering how many of them were around or if they were out on assignment.

Gotta hurry.

Two hours wasn't much time to track down fifteen demons that Beltine knew and trusted who would work well together, and he had no intention of failing his master.

Chapter Two

Something is off. Something is going on.
Like some sixth sense, Kavan just knew it. He'd lost track of how long he'd been trapped in his animal form by the witches. At first, he'd tried to escape, but every attempt had failed, resulting in whippings and starvation.

Kavan had finally accepted the inevitable — without help — he wasn't going anywhere.

Once Kavan had stopped fighting them, his life had turned into one of monotony. He knew the day of the week by who fed him and when someone came to draw his blood.

Except, the woman who had been drawing his blood every Thursday for who knew how long hadn't shown. The people who fed him were wrong, too. In all his time in the zoo-like cage, an acolyte had never done the feeding . . . until the prior Saturday.

Now, all his feedings were done by the men and women who followed the witches in the Dawn of Time circle.

Lifting his head from the feeder containing his hay, Kavan flicked his ears and panned his gaze slowly around the area. He checked each cage he could see, but he saw nothing amiss. All the other shifters equally trapped were either sleeping or eating.

As a giraffe, Kavan had no trouble seeing through the dim light of twilight. His nearly twenty-foot height allowed him to make out almost every inch of the exotic animal rescue facility — *Dawn of Time Animal Rescue*, according to the sign near the road anyway. There were three acolytes pushing around

9

cleaning tools, moving between cages. Another pair stood near the front office, whispering together. From the tension in both women's shoulders, Kavan knew he wasn't the only one who thought something was going on.

Could this be it? Could this be the chance I need to get away?

Having been docile for years, Kavan had watched how the people around him had grown lax in their diligence of his security. He'd even seen one man leave his cage unlatched. Unfortunately, Kavan hadn't been able to shift so he could fit through the human-sized door.

Too bad.

So, Kavan continued to bide his time.

A moving shadow out of the corner of his eye caught Kavan's attention. He turned his head and stared, waiting to see if it happened again. For several long minutes, nothing happened. Then . . . it did.

Chaos erupted.

Women and men screamed as winged creatures leaped from the shadows. Their slender, milky-white bodies were human-shaped with claws on their hands and feet. They sported large, bat-like wings and wore pale-gray leather leggings. They wielded their wings as weapons just as much as their hands and feet, knocking the acolytes nearest to them to the ground.

Four security personnel burst from the office. They began shooting at the beasts, and everyone else ran or dove for cover.

Pain stabbed through Kavan's thigh.

Stumbling to the right, Kavan did his best to hide his large body behind the grotto that offered him shade during the day. He peeked his head around the side and watched as several of the white, winged creatures dispatched each shooter. There had to be over a dozen of them, and they easily ferreted out each of the hiding men and women.

Kavan waited, watching, wondering who they were and

what they planned. His heart thudded swiftly in his chest as he felt his blood drip down his leg.

When one of the creatures who carried an unconscious security officer over his shoulder walked past Kavan's cage, he sniffed the air and paused. He peered in at him and frowned. Then his gaze seemed to zero in on Kavan's leg.

"Well, damn, buddy. I'm sorry." The creature patted the head of the man he held, and it didn't look too gentle. "These assholes didn't care where they shot, did they? I'll let my commander know, and we'll get you looked at before we leave."

Gaping, even in animal form — *holy crap, the creatures are intelligent* — Kavan stared, shocked.

The beast grinned broadly, showing off a mouthful of sharp teeth. "Ah, you're a shifter, and you totally don't know what we are, do you?"

Taking a chance — hell, his situation couldn't get much worse, in his opinion — Kavan slowly shook his head.

Standing proudly, the male used a clawed thumb to point at his chest. "We're demons. We're here making certain none of the witches in this circle escaped us and cleaning up their followers." Snorting derisively, he added, "Not like last time." Cocking his head, he asked, "Can you shift?"

Once more, Kavan shook his head.

"You stuck like that?"

Kavan hated to think it was permanent, but he just didn't know, so he nodded. Currently, he was indeed stuck in his giraffe form.

"All right." The creature — demon — *wow* — glanced around. "I guess all these could be shifters. Pretty good cover, an exotic animal rescue. No one would question why they'd draw your blood." Then the demon refocused on Kavan. "Okay. Sit tight, buddy. My commander will know what to do."

Then the demon trotted away.

As if I can do anything else.

Turning his head slowly, worried about becoming dizzy,

Kavan spotted the wound high up on his thigh. He fought the animalistic urge to lick it. With a sigh, he returned to watching the goings-on.

The demons scurried this way and that. They rounded up all the humans and took them into the front square. All of the conscious ones were forced onto their knees with their hands on their heads.

Another demon rounded a building with a male that appeared human beside him. The man was equally pale, with long white hair. His ice-blue eyes swept over the group as he listened to whatever the demon was telling him.

They began walking amongst those they'd captured, and Kavan found his gaze riveted on the demon. Just like the others, his body was pale, and his wings were massive and bat-like. While Kavan couldn't say what it was that made him different, he felt an urge to brush the demon's thick hair over his shoulder so he could trace down the pale column of his neck.

Huh. That's a weird thought.

Tugging his focus away from the sexy demon — *also a weird thought* — Kavan watched the human-looking guy. He would tip a human's chin up and look into their eyes. As Kavan stared, he noticed that the guy's blue eyes appeared to glimmer in the moonlight.

Okay. Not human. What is he?

Kavan had met vampires a few times, but he knew that when they used their mind-powers, their eyes turned red. They certainly didn't appear to glow. Plus, the guy seemed to be the boss of a squad of demons.

A fissure of worry slithered up Kavan's spine.

What's going on?

Kavan tried to remind himself that the demon who'd talked to him had seemed nice enough. He'd reassured Kavan that he would be taken care of. That didn't mean killed, did it?

As Kavan watched, the demon who'd stopped to speak

with him laid the man he'd been carrying onto the sidewalk. He even appeared to do it with a considerable amount of care. Then he stopped next to the pair and said something to them.

Both the human-looking guy and the handsome demon looked Kavan's way. The head honcho murmured something, and the sexy demon nodded. Then the winged male beckoned for the guy that Kavan had met to follow him.

The pair started in Kavan's direction.

Kavan found himself transfixed as the handsome demon drew closer. The way he walked with such confidence was a turn-on. He had his wings lifted partway, and the appendages billowed in the evening breeze, making Kavan wonder what they would feel like beneath his fingers.

Too bad I can't shift.

Just outside one of Kavan's gates, the handsome demon stopped. His nostrils flared, and he cocked his head. Slowly, his lips parted as an expression of shock took over his features.

"Beltine?" the other demon asked, frowning in obvious concern. "Is something wrong?"

"I-I'm not certain, Consifen," Beltine replied, still looking a little shell-shocked. "His blood."

Consifen reached for the door lock and broke it. "Hell, I know this isn't the first time you've scented blood, Bels." Pulling the door open, he started through, adding, "What about it?"

"It calls to me," Beltine replied, seeming to move forward as if on autopilot. His ice-blue eyes remained wide as he swept his gaze over Kavan over and over. "As if he were my *amina*."

Freezing, Consifen gaped . . . but only for an instant. "Your *amina*? Holy shit!" He grinned broadly, showing off all his pointed teeth. "That's fantastic. Congratulations!"

Beltine turned his shell-shocked gaze onto Consifen. "But I still have over two decades until my thousandth birthday."

Consifen's joy faded to be replaced by his own look of confusion. "But, then . . . are you sure?"

"I, uh—" Beltine returned his attention to Kavan. "Not totally, but I've never felt the desire to lick away a person's blood before."

Kavan wished he could ask the demons what the hell they were talking about. Lowering his head, he stretched his neck toward the pair as he took a limping step toward them. He hoped to get their attention . . . maybe figure out a way to ask them to explain what an *amina* was.

With his head so much closer to the pair, Kavan finally smelled something other than his own blood. The metallic and earthy goodness teased his senses, causing his mouth to water. For the first time in his life, Kavan felt his cock threaten to swell while in animal form.

What the hell?

Taking another step, Kavan brought his head closer to the staring pair. He easily parsed which demon smelled so delicious—Beltine. The fact that the male had drawn his interest made so much more sense.

As odd as Kavan found it, Beltine—a demon—was his mate. He wondered what a demon even was. How had he never heard about their kind?

Kavan supposed he was considered young by shifter standards. While he hadn't had access to a calendar in a long time, he guessed he had to have entered his eightieth decade by now. He hadn't held a rank in his herd, either, having just been a run-of-the-mill member.

Maybe that's why I was never rescued.

His family had little sway with the decisions made by the alpha and his inner circle.

Instead, I'm being rescued by my mate and his people . . . whoever they may be. Oh, maybe that's what amina *means? But what does his age have to do with it? And holy hell. Was he really talking about being a thousand years old?*

The sound of Consifen's chuckle drew Kavan out of his musings . . . and he realized that he'd begun to rub his muzzle against Beltine's chest.

"Guess he thinks you're his *amina,* too," Consifen stated with amusement.

"A shifter calls it a mate," Beltine murmured, sounding shocked. Gently, he rested his clawed hands on either side of Kavan's face. Softly, he asked, "Do you think I'm your mate, giraffe?"

Peering into the male's ice-blue eyes, Kavan saw confusion and a hint of concern, but there was hope in there, too. Vocalizing softly, he nodded once before returning to nuzzling his furred cheek against Beltine's torso. He wanted his scent all over the male.

Beltine didn't seem to mind, rubbing over his cheek, head, and neck with surprising gentleness considering how his fingers ended in claws.

"Okay, so, this is unexpected," Beltine murmured, continuing to touch him. "And Consifen said you can't shift?"

Shaking his head just a smidge, Kavan confirmed what Consifen had relayed.

Beltine hummed as he nodded. "Gods, it would suck if you were stuck in your animal form for two decades," he whispered.

Kavan had no idea how to question that.

"All right, handsome," Beltine rumbled as he gently petted the skin between Kavan's nostrils. "We need to take a look at your leg. Will you let us?"

Nuzzling Beltine had distracted Kavan from his pain, but with his mate's words, the pulsing waves of unpleasantness returned in full force.

Rumbling unhappily, Kavan turned his head and peered at his injured limb.

"Let's take that as a yes," Consifen stated. Patting Beltine

15

on the shoulder, he urged, "Why don't you keep petting him, Bels. It seems to distract him."

"I can do that," Beltine replied agreeably. At the same time, he used light touches to urge Kavan to refocus on him. "Check it out, Cons. Let me know what's needed to help him."

"You got it."

Consifen then headed toward Kavan's injured limb.

Kavan decided to focus on Beltine's scent when the demon began poking and prodding.

CHAPTER THREE

Beltine's mind reeled.

No way should this have happened.

While Beltine had heard the rumors that shifters found their mates when one or both needed them, he didn't think that applied to his kind. After all, demons were assigned an *amina* after one thousand years of service. Beltine couldn't think of one instance where that hadn't been the case.

Then Beltine recalled how demons from all four horsemen had been captured and killed for their blood. From what he understood, blood magick was dangerous under normal circumstances. Using demon blood made the spells far more powerful, but it had the side effect of impacting the Moirai, too.

Is this a situation like that?

After all, Beltine knew that Famine would have helped every shifter there even if none of them were a demon's *amina*.

Is there actually a better choice out there for the giraffe?

As swiftly as that thought entered Beltine's head, a possessiveness unlike anything he'd ever felt before flooded his body. He wanted to slip through the mists and take his shifter to the demon realm. Hiding him away from everyone else until Beltine could bond with him sounded like the best damn idea ever.

A low moaning noise yanked Beltine back to the present . . . and what he was supposed to be doing.

Right. Distract the giraffe.

"Well, I wish I knew your name," Beltine began slowly as

he rubbed the backs of his fingers over the giraffe's furred cheek. "But since I don't, I'll leave it at handsome." With a wink, he rumbled, "I'm sure you will be in human form, too."

The giraffe's deep amber eyes stared at him, hints of pain swirling within their depths.

"Well, what can I do to distract you," Beltine mused. What he wanted to do could only be done if the shifter had been in human form. *Too bad.* "Let's see." Beltine racked his brain for something.

"I don't think he knows about demons, Bels," Consifen stated from where he was inspecting the giraffe's haunch.

Beltine rubbed the giraffe's forehead before teasing up to one of his horns. He knew the animals came in different breeds, and he wondered what his *amina* was. His brown splotches and white patterning were fascinating.

"Do you know about demons?" Beltine asked, staring into one of the giraffe's large eyes. He felt the shifter shake his head ever-so-slightly. "Okay," he began slowly. "Well, that could be because we live on a different plane than this one. We travel here through magickal corridors called lei lines in order to fulfill the duties assigned to us by the Four Horsemen of the Apocalypse."

To Beltine's surprise, the giraffe pulled away and snorted. The beast's eyes widened as it back up a step. Even in animal form, Beltine could see the shifter's alarm, and the acrid scent burned his sensitive nostrils.

"Easy, easy," Beltine crooned, sorting through what he could have said to upset his *amina*. Realizing what it could have been, he wanted to kick himself. "We don't capture shifters or use their blood as spells. Demons *are* magick. We don't need help to perform our abilities." Seeing the giraffe's continued upset, Beltine lifted his hands in placation. "Please, handsome. I would never hurt you." Wincing, he added, "Other than the soul-bonding." Beltine lifted a finger, asking for patience. "Which I will explain. Demons are a little different than the paranormals on this plane."

Beltine took a chance and flapped his wings. With a few quick pumps, he hovered before his giraffe's head. "Easy, baby," he crooned, gently taking the male's snout between his hands. "I'm your mate, remember? Just because I use a different word, I still consider you a gift from the Fates. I'll do everything in my power to make this work between us."

To Beltine's relief, as the giraffe stared at him, he blinked slowly. Some of the tension eased from the animal's features. He rumbled softly in a clearly questioning vocalization.

Beltine really wished he understood giraffe.

Smiling, Beltine continued to flap his wings, holding himself as steady as possible. He rubbed his *amina*'s furry cheeks. At the same time, Beltine leaned forward and pressed a kiss to his shifter's nose.

"So, yes . . . demons are different than shifters or vampires or gargoyles," Beltine began again. He realized he needed to clarify a bit more. "Demons are not born," he explained. "We are created by the gods. At that time, we are assigned to one of the Four Horsemen of the Apocalypse." Smirking upon seeing the clear question in the giraffe's eyes, Beltine winked. "Yes, they are real."

His shifter huffed a disbelieving-sounding sigh before nodding once.

"So, anyway." *Where was I? Right.* "The Four Horsemen send their demons to this realm in order to carry out tasks ordered by the gods with the goal of keeping humans and their place on the earth in balance." Grimacing, Beltine admitted, "Sometimes, that requires humans and other paranormals to experience war, famine, pestilence, and of course, death. It's the cycle of life."

After a few seconds, the giraffe bobbed his head in a slight nod.

Relief flooded Beltine.

Okay. That's a step forward.

Hopefully . . .

"So, I said we're created and assigned to our horseman," Beltine continued, hoping his *amina* would understand. Some other paranormals had a prejudice against their kind, so as difficult as explaining was, he sort of appreciated it. "I'm a demon under the Horseman of Famine." Chuckling softly, Beltine admitted, "Normally, I'm sent somewhere to cause a drought or something, so this is actually a nice change for me."

Beltine believed he could see the question in the shifter's amber eyes, so he explained, "We're here to confirm that this circle of witches has been completely wiped out as well as clear out who they've been affiliating with. They're using blood magick that's creating ripple effects causing problems on many planes of existence and must be stopped. We're also trying to track down the book of spells that gave them this knowledge."

For a few seconds, the giraffe worked his jaw, as if he were frustrated about not being able to ask something — well, probably a great many things. Then he bleated oddly and swung his head toward his leg . . . and Consifen. His annoyance and pain could easily be read.

"Easy, handsome," Beltine called, reaching for the giraffe's head. He rubbed soothingly. "Let's see what Cons has to say, huh?"

Huffing, the giraffe just stared at him balefully.

"Cons?" Beltine asked. "How's it lookin' there?"

Beltine hated that any of the shifters had been injured while they were cleaning house. The fact that it was his *amina* made it ten times worse. He hoped he heard from Kender soon, as he was the leader of the team he'd put in charge of inventorying and checking the other animals in the fake exotic rescue.

Are they all shifters?

"Not so good, Beltine," Consifen replied. Leaving the shifter's leg, he flew over and hovered beside Beltine near the giraffe's head. "I'm real sorry, buddy." Grimacing, Consifen explained, "The bullet is lodged in the flesh of your haunch. It's going to be a little painful for me to dig it out." Then the demon held his hand palm up and chanted a spell in the harsh guttural demon language. A second later, several sets of long, thin tweezers of various sizes lay across his palm. "But I'll be as careful as possible."

The giraffe jerked backward again, staring at Consifen in alarm. He glanced between them both as he backed up one step, then two.

"Easy, handsome," Beltine rumbled again, holding up his hands in placation. "I told you. Demons are magick. We don't need blood or anything. It's already within us." Closing the distance between them once again, Beltine did his best to re-assure his *amina*. "You have nothing to fear from any of us. I would never allow anyone to hurt you" — wincing, he fin-ished — "as much as possible." Then Beltine directed a pointed look in Consifen's direction.

Consifen nodded, his expression serious. "Yes, Beltine." Focusing on the giraffe, he offered, "I'll be as careful as I can." Then he smiled in reassurance. "Have Beltine explain soul-bonding to you. That'll be a good distraction."

Wincing, Beltine nodded. "I fear you're right."

Nodding, Consifen headed back toward the giraffe's haunch. "Okay, big guy. Try to stay perfectly still." Then he paused. "Would it be easier to lie down?"

The giraffe sighed before shaking his head.

Beltine would have to ask about that later. Did giraffes not lie down? He didn't actually know anything about the ani-mal's habits other than them being herbivores, which ex-plained the grasses in his hay feeder.

"Okay, then," Beltine began slowly. "Bonding with a demon is a little different than mating with another shifter. More involved." Seeing he had his shifter's attention, Beltine continued, "Like I said, we're created, not born, so we don't have souls. Instead, our existence is bound to our master. To break that attachment, we bind with our *amina*, instead, sharing their soul with them for eternity."

Seeing he had the giraffe's undivided attention, Beltine hated what he needed to share next. "It's done by you verbally offering three things to me — your blood, your body, and your soul." When the giraffe winced, Beltine rubbed his palms over his face, soothing as best he could. "Everything is traditionally done through sex, and the first two are simple enough. I'm sorry to say that the process of you sharing your soul with me, binding us forever, is indeed painful for you." Knowing he needed to be honest, Beltine added, "And the soul-tearing ritual must be done four times, each causing a greater amount of pain. I'll do everything I can to distract you, causing you as much pleasure as possible to counter it. I — "

"Beltine, why are you explaining demon bonding and soul-tearing to this shifter?" Famine's voice cut into Beltine's explanation. "He scents to be getting quite upset."

"Master Famine." Keeping one hand on the giraffe's cheek, rubbing lightly, Beltine turned in the air to face his master. "I'm trying to distract my *amina* from Consifen working the bullet out of his haunch." Growling softly, he added, "If I figure out which of those damn guards shot him, I'm going to — "

"Your *amina*?" Once again, Master Famine cut into his diatribe, which was probably for the best. "But you're — "

Famine stopped, his eyes widening. In the next instant, he pulled his shirt from his torso before unfurling his pale blue wings. He rose in the air until he was level with Beltine and the giraffe's head.

"You're right," Famine murmured, his blue eyes gleaming as if he saw something Beltine didn't—which he probably did. "I do see the lines of connection between you." Then Famine blinked, and the glow was gone. He focused on Beltine, his brows creasing in concern. "This is an unexpected complication. You still have over two decades to go."

Beltine grimaced. "I know. Is there"—he licked his lips, worry and hope warring within him—"any way to bond early?"

Famine cleared his throat, looking distinctly uncomfortable. "I will . . . need to speak with my brothers."

With his hope increasing, Beltine nodded. After all, that wasn't a *no*. "Thank you, Master Famine."

"You're welcome, Beltine," Famine replied softly, eyeing the shifter. "In the meantime, we have two options. All the shifters should be taken somewhere to have their blood drawn."

The giraffe grunted and shifted his weight, expressing his displeasure.

"Hold still, buddy," Consifen called. "Almost done."

Huffing, the shifter settled.

"It would be to figure out what in your blood is stopping you from shifting," Beltine hurried to explain. "Others have run into this and know how to counter it." With a shrug, he added, "Otherwise, it's just a waiting game. What they gave to you could be permanent without treatment, or it could wear off within a week or two."

"It's your choice, handsome," Beltine assured. "I would never take that away from you."

CHAPTER FOUR

In the end, Kavan had gotten his point across. He hadn't wanted any more of his blood drawn, choosing option two to start with. Considering he'd been in his animal form for years, another possible week or two felt like seeing the light at the end of the tunnel.

Beltine had agreed that, if Kavan didn't successfully shift within a couple of weeks, then they would pursue the treatment option.

Kavan really hoped it didn't come to that. He'd had more than his fair share of being stuck with needles. As much as Kavan wanted his mate — to communicate with him, to hold him, and to touch him — he could be patient.

After all, according to Beltine, they would have eternity together.

Plus, it gave Kavan a little time to come to terms with everything that Beltine had told him.

While Kavan had openly scented Beltine as he'd explained demons and their culture, he still had a hard time believing him. The idea of other planes of existence blew his mind. He wanted to ask about that, see if the demon knew how many planes there actually were. Were there even more creatures and beings out there? Then Beltine had shared soul-bonding.

Holy shit! I'll definitely be asking about that after I shift.

Kavan had to keep up his hope that whatever the witches had been giving him *would* wear off.

"Are you ready to leave, handsome?"

Looking from Beltine to his still-locked, animal-sized door,

Kavan cocked his head. He didn't relish the idea of limping anywhere, but to get out of the zoo, he would most definitely deal with the pain.

Beltine smiled. "We won't be leaving that way." With a wink, he added, "We'll be going the demon way." Beltine peered beyond Kavan. "You finished, Consifen?"

Consifen patted Kavan's belly gently. "All set." He flapped his wings and moved toward his head. "The bullet is out. I know you guys heal fast, but I magicked up a bandage for it anyway." Then Consifen turned a cheeky grin Beltine's way. "Too bad he can't offer you his blood. You could lick up his blood, sealing the wound and starting your bond all at the same time."

Frowning at Consifen, Beltine grumbled, "Yes, too bad."

Kavan bumped his head into Beltine's arm, then nuzzled against his shoulder.

Beltine smiled at him, his ire with his fellow demon melting away. "I'll get you some place where you can doze and rest in peace."

"If you intend to take him through the mists, I think you should have a few friends ready to catch him in case he passes out." Famine cocked his head with his arms crossed over his lean torso. "Unless you know a levitation spell?"

"Oh, right," Beltine murmured, nodding at Famine. "Thank you, Master Famine. Good idea." Casting a concerned look Kavan's way, he explained, "Most non-demons pass out the first few times they pass from this plane to the demon realm. Just in case you do, too, I'm going to use a spell to carry you. I wouldn't want you toppling over onto your injury." Floating backward, Beltine put a little space between them. "This is going to feel a little weird, but I won't let you fall. Do you trust me?"

As much as Kavan wanted to ask what Beltine was going to do, he couldn't. Instead, he dipped his head in a small nod.

"Okay. Here we go."

Beltine began speaking in what Kavan was beginning to recognize as his native tongue.

"Come, Consifen. We have a few more things to attend to," Famine ordered just as Beltine finished speaking.

An odd weightlessness crept through Kavan's body, and he felt as if he were floating. The strange sensation yanked a surprised bleat from him. He looked at the ground, but it appeared as if he was still standing. It just didn't feel like it.

"Relax, my *amina*," Beltine encouraged. "You're safe. You're fine."

Kavan could do little but trust in Beltine. Once again, he was under someone else's command. His heart pounded with discomfort even as he tried to will his body into relaxing.

"Get moving, Beltine," Famine ordered. "He's not liking that."

"Yes, Master Famine."

After those words, Beltine rested his hand on Kavan's shoulder, and he didn't remember anything after that.

"Good morning, handsome. How are you feeling this morning?"

Kavan had watched Beltine's eyelids flutter open. The demon had taken to sleeping under the trees with him, even though he had a suite in the palace. It was on the second floor, with a balcony, and Beltine had opened the French doors and allowed Kavan to stick his head in so he could see the place.

In truth, the gorgeously appointed rooms had been far nicer than his home back on herd-lands—his parents and alpha's, too.

Beltine had explained that everything had been created by Famine and magick. There was no cost for anything, and the horseman gave his minions the best of everything. Of course, that didn't mean the demons didn't earn it. Beltine had shown him training grounds and schooling halls where they learned to fight and wield their magick.

Demons didn't have a life in the traditional sense. When they were created, they were small and shaped a lot like monkeys, and they didn't have wings. Year after year, their bodies changed, becoming more humanoid and muscular. A knowledgeable person could guess a demon's age by their body shape and the size of their wings.

As Kavan peered down at Beltine, he admired the demon's wings. They were massive white appendages and felt like buttery soft leather against the fine hairs of his muzzle. He enjoyed rubbing them, and Beltine seemed to like it, too, often humming appreciatively.

"Handsome?"

Kavan realized he hadn't truly acknowledged Beltine's greeting. Lowering his head, he rubbed the side of his muzzle against Beltine's upper arm affectionately. When the demon immediately petted him, Kavan sighed with pleasure.

Not for the first time, Kavan wondered what those clawed hands would feel like on his human skin. His mate was always careful, never scratching him. If he were in human form, he didn't think he would mind a little extra stimulation from them.

The notion of Beltine scraping his skin drew a soft sigh of desire from Kavan, even in giraffe form. It had been nearly two weeks, and being in proximity to the male but not being able to do anything about it was getting old. Kavan wanted human hands to touch and explore the muscular male reclining on the grass beneath his hooves.

To Kavan's shock, he felt his body respond. His limbs trembled as the muscles under his skin rippled. He felt his neck ache as it began to meld together, shortening. As his fur started retracting into his skin, tingles spread over his body, and not the good kind.

Kavan couldn't remember the last time fiery pain accompanied his shift. Still, he embraced it because he knew it would be worth it in the end. He did his best to relax as he crashed to the ground on his belly, a deep groan escaping him.

As his shift drew to an end, Kavan became aware of Beltine's hand on his back, sliding up and down his spine. He hummed appreciatively upon feeling the gentle touch. With a sigh, Kavan remained still as the residual echoes of pain eased from his frame.

"Handsome?" Beltine murmured uncertainly. "Are you okay?" His breath wafted over Kavan's ear, causing the hairs on his nape to stand on end as Beltine continued, "I know shifters say that changing form feels like a good stretch after sitting for too long, but that really sounded painful."

Kavan finally gathered enough energy and turned his head. Smiling at Beltine, he whispered, "Hi, Beltine. I'm Kavan." His voice came out rough from disuse, and he swallowed hard, trying to get some moisture to it.

"Hi, Kavan." Beltine curled against his side. Slinging a leg over his ass, he rested his head on his arm as he lay next to him. "You didn't answer my question, my *amina*. How are you feeling?"

"Never better," Kavan replied. After swallowing again, he admitted, "Unless I had a glass of water."

Beltine chuckled softly. "I can do that for you." Then he rolled away from Kavan, rising to a sitting position. Holding one hand palm up, he whispered a few words in his demon tongue. Instantly, a wooden mug appeared in his hand. Turning back to Kavan, Beltine asked, "Can I help you sit up?"

Kavan almost denied the demon. Except, as he began pushing with his limbs, he realized he had no strength. With a sigh, Kavan nodded.

After setting the mug in the grass, Beltine reached for Kavan. He carefully maneuvered around him while helping him roll and sit up. In just a few seconds, Kavan found himself with his back to Beltine's chest while the demon leaned against a tree.

While rubbing up and down his side, Beltine picked the mug back up. "Here you go." He brought it to Kavan's lips. "Small sips. So, I'm going with that was pretty damn painful."

With shaking hands, Kavan gripped the mug, but Beltine didn't release it. He accepted the aid and took one small sip after another. Cool, clean water flowed across his tongue, tasting like the best thing he could ever remember. While Kavan had access to water in a nearby stream Beltine had shown him, giraffe's obtained most of their moisture from their food. With the way Kavan had to spread his front legs to drink, it was awkward and uncomfortable, and he tended to avoid it. There was something to be said for using a mug while in human form.

Plus, it's been so long.

"Yes," Kavan admitted, once he'd lowered the mug to his chest. He sighed and relaxed against the broader male. "Hasn't felt like that since the first couple of times." Closing his eyes, Kavan rested his head on Beltine's shoulder and whispered, "Shifting is like a muscle. If you don't use it, it atrophies. Then the first couple of times you start doing it again, it hurts. That's why kids are encouraged to do it often."

"Ah, that makes sense," Beltine murmured.

Kavan registered the unmistakable feel of lips on his neck, and he hummed as he turned his head to offer more encouragement.

Beltine took the offer at face value. Sliding his arms around Kavan's waist, he skimmed his claws ever-so-lightly along the lines of his ribcage. At the same time, Beltine began working the sensitive skin along the column of what he knew was considered a long neck for a human.

"I've been wondering what you would look like in human form," Beltine mumbled, his words a little hard to make out since he didn't lift his head. "You're gorgeous, although I'd love to see a little more weight on you."

Enjoying the tingles that Beltine's touches created, Kavan wasn't offended in the least by his words. He knew he was underweight. In the wild, a giraffe his size could easily eat one-hundred-fifty pounds of leaves and shoots a day. As a shifter, he had an even larger appetite. The witches weren't offering him nearly that much.

With a soft chuckle, Kavan mumbled, "If you give me food, I'll eat it." Of course, with the way his blood flowed swiftly to his groin in response to Beltine's light strokes over his stomach and sides, Kavan wanted something other than food so much more. "But later. Touch me," he demanded.

"Anything you want," Beltine replied, a soft growl in his voice. "Just relax and let me please you."

Then, to Kavan's delight, Beltine did just that.

Beltine wrapped his long, strong fingers around his erection and began stroking strongly. His other hand slipped to cradle Kavan's balls, and he rolled them gently, stimulating him. Beltine sucked on his neck, most likely working up a mark, and Kavan didn't mind one bit.

Kavan didn't bother fighting it as his body fired hot with arousal, and the need to come swelled swiftly. He didn't know if it was due to not finding release in so damn long or if it was because this was his mate, but he was on the brink in seconds. Groaning Beltine's name, Kavan fell over the edge.

His body jerked in Beltine's hold as his orgasm washed over him, relaxing him and sending him soaring all at the same time.

Needing to please his lover in some fashion, too—and considering the way Beltine worked his neck—Kavan whispered, "Beltine, I offer you my blood."

The groan Beltine rumbled against his throat was nearly as satisfying as the sensation of the demon's bite.

CHAPTER FIVE

Beltine heard Kavan's words and groaned. Unable to help himself, he took what his *amina* offered. He sank his sharp teeth into the slender column of flesh, piercing his skin deeply.

Blood welled up around his teeth, and Beltine sucked once, twice, before easing his teeth free. He moaned again as the flavor of his shifter's blood flowed across his taste buds. Beltine suckled, enjoying another mouthful.

The taste of his *amina* on Beltine's tongue was like nothing he'd ever experienced. The scent of his shifter's cum flooding the air was the greatest aphrodisiac he'd ever enjoyed. Those things combined with his inner sense of satisfaction upon feeling the first formation of their bond.

Beltine's own arousal erupted in his veins like a flash fire in a hot pan. His cock swelled so fast it made his head spin. Before he could even hope to control himself, Beltine came, unloading his seed into the crotch of his leather pants.

Panting roughly through his nose, Beltine finally came back to himself. He hummed as he lapped at Kavan's neck, sealing his bonding mark so it no longer bled. Considering how his shifter had responded to his bite, Beltine intended to reopen that mark over and over.

"Hmmm," Kavan mumbled, turning his head and staring up at him with a loopy expression. "That was amazing. Can't wait for you to fuck me."

Beltine grinned at Kavan even as he felt his cock twitch

with renewed interest at that idea. Having been around Kavan for the past couple of weeks while he was in animal form hadn't been too bad. The second his *amina* had returned to human form, however, Beltine had been slammed with unfamiliar instincts — the need to claim and possess.

Kavan is mine, and now that I've marked him, everyone will know.

Mine.

Admiring the man relaxing in his arms, Beltine spotted the pale, creamy essence splashed across his torso. He rested one hand on Kavan's thigh, using his thumb-claw to tease into the crease of his groin, continuing to stimulate his lover. With his other hand, Beltine swiped two forefingers through a large glob.

Beltine brought it to his lips and licked the cream from his digits. The flavor was saltier than he'd expected, but he didn't mind one bit. He loved salt, always adding extra to his food.

"You're perfect," Beltine mumbled, pleased beyond measure. "I—"

Pausing, Beltine listened as Kavan's stomach growled. In hindsight, sex the second his *amina* shifted for the first time probably hadn't been the best idea. Still, his shifter had been in need, had expressed his desire, and Beltine had been helpless to resist.

"Time for breakfast," Beltine stated, shifting their weight forward a bit. Feeling the wetness in his groin, he added, "And to get cleaned up. Breakfast and a hot bath."

As Beltine slowly rose, using his wings for a little extra lift, he slid his arms around Kavan and cradled him to his chest.

"Mmm, I could walk, you know," Kavan offered the half-hearted resistance, but he didn't try to get away from him.

"Perhaps," Beltine conceded. "But why tire yourself when you don't need to?" He then draped his wings around them, hiding Kavan's nudity from view. "Plus, this way, I can do this."

Kavan chuckled softly as he petted the wing draped over him. "I love your wings."

Beltine grinned, pleased. "I like that you pet them," he admitted. It felt so damn good to be accepted as he was.

Relaxing against Beltine, Kavan murmured, "Thank you for saving me, for caring for me, for being so patient." He lifted his right arm and rubbed the side of his neck. "I know the needle marks don't show because I'm a shifter, but sometimes, I feel like the needle is still in there." Kavan's voice lowered, becoming strained. "They took it every week, like clockwork, until a week before you rescued everyone."

"You're welcome, Kavan," Beltine replied seriously. "Even if you hadn't been my *amina*, we would still have helped each and every one of you."

Beltine referred to the five other shifters that had been in captivity. There had been a number of true animals, too, probably to keep up appearances. Over the course of the couple of weeks he'd been hanging out with his *amina*'s giraffe, he'd explained that the other shifters included an elephant, a camel, a gray wolf, a capybara, and a coral snake.

Kavan smiled up at him. "I know."

Pressing a quick kiss to Kavan's temple, Beltine murmured, "You never have to worry about that again."

"Thank you," Kavan repeated. After clearing his throat, he asked, "So, what's first? Food or bath?" He grimaced, adding, "I'm definitely hungry, but gods, the idea of being clean is so very appealing."

"Then we'll do both," Beltine stated with a wink. Spotting a fellow demon, he hollered, "Consifen! Come here, man."

Consifen whirled where he'd been heading down a side hall. Spotting the man in his arms, his pale lips curved into a wide grin. He jogged toward them, his expression never waning.

"Hey, Bels," Consifen greeted, sweeping his gaze over the

wing-draped Kavan. "Who do we have here?"

Grinning broadly, Beltine introduced, "This is my *amina*, Kavan."

"Good to finally meet you properly, Kavan." Consifen dipped his head, but he didn't offer his hand. "I'm happy for you both." With a wink, Consifen pointed at the mark Beltine had left on Kavan's neck. "Got started already, huh? Did Master Famine get back to you about how to finish the bond early?"

"Thank you, and not yet," Beltine admitted. Considering until just that morning Kavan had been in giraffe form, it hadn't been too pressing on his mind. He'd been more interested in making certain Kavan healed properly and felt comfortable in the demon realm. "I'll touch base with him about it this afternoon, but I was hoping to ask a favor of you."

Slipping his thumbs into the waistband of his leather pants, Consifen cocked his head. "If I can. What's up?"

"Will you bring a cart of food up to my suite?" Beltine requested. "My *amina* could use a good meal as well as a bath."

"Ahhh, of course." Consifen focused on Kavan. "Any favorites I should be aware of?"

Kavan opened his mouth, then closed it again. His cheeks flushed a little as he admitted, "I'd love just about anything other than a salad."

Consifen barked a laugh even as he nodded. "You got it. I'll bring a variety," he promised. As he headed toward their community dining hall, Consifen called over his shoulder, "I'll knock on the door and leave it in the hall for you. See you later."

"Thanks, Cons," Beltine replied before heading deeper into the palace. "I know I told you there's over a dozen wings," he reminded his *amina*. "We're in the emerald wing." Beltine used his chin to indicate the trim near the ceiling that had been decorated in massive amounts of deep green emeralds.

"The only time a demon goes into a different wing is if they're invited or ordered."

Kavan nodded. "Got it." His gaze seemed riveted on the trim. "Wow," he whispered. "That's a lot of emeralds."

"Is it?" Beltine eyed the decoration. Then it occurred to him that maybe humans valued the pretty gems differently than demons. After all, Beltine had seen them on jewelry. "Are they worth much? Master Famine created them with a wave of his hand."

Scoffing, Kavan told him, "There are those who would kill their own mother for just a fraction of the wealth on the walls of this wing alone." Kavan focused on Beltine with wide hazel eyes. "Don't ever let a circle of witches know about this," he warned. "They were always complaining about not having enough money. Hell, even some paranormal groups would give their right arm for it."

Beltine nodded. "I'll spread that warning."

Reaching his suite, Beltine uncurled an arm just enough to grip the latch and open his door. He entered, then used his foot to close the door behind him. Moving through the lushly appointed room, Beltine headed into his private bathing chamber.

Hearing Kavan's gasp, Beltine focused on his face and scent, reading his delight. He looked over the room, trying to assess it from his *amina's* point of view. Considering his shifter had been trapped as a giraffe for who knew how long, Beltine would guess that it wouldn't take much.

As was standard, a deep stone pool was embedded in the floor with steps leading into it. The oval basin had taps at the deeper end allowing for it to be filled with water. There were seats carved out along various points in the side, giving a person options on how deeply they wished to recline in the water. There were even pipes running around certain points that would pump heated air into the bath, similar to a hot tub in the human realm.

"Gods," Kavan murmured in obvious appreciation. "This is fantastic. It looks so relaxing for strained muscles."

"It is." Beltine knew from experience. "Let's get you in." He started down the stairs, heading into the tub. "I'm going to put you on a step that should put the water level about mid-chest."

Gently, Beltine placed his *amina* in what he knew was a comfortable seat, despite being made of stone. He started the water, positioning the taps to the heat level he preferred. Glancing over his shoulder, Beltine hoped his shifter liked it similar, but he would be happy to change for the man who held his soul.

Taking in Kavan's position, Beltine admired his shifter. While he hadn't seen the male stand up, he guessed him to be almost as tall as his own six-foot-six height due to his long, slender limbs. His frame was much slimmer, however — gaunt, almost, from malnutrition — but he bet once his *amina* was fed up, he would have lean muscles and strong lines.

Can't wait to help him with that.

Beltine also remembered the whip scars he'd seen on Kavan's back, flanks, and legs when he'd been petting up and down his spine earlier.

Never again will he endure such pain.

Beltine found himself lingering over his new and forever lover's face the most, however. He'd pushed his shaggy, medium-brown hair behind his ears, probably trying to tame the unkempt locks. His eyes were a deep hazel, bordering on gold — amber, similar to his animal. Stress and fatigue lines creased Kavan's forehead as he swept his gaze around the place, wariness and hopefulness battling within him — judging by the scents he was giving off.

"If you want the water hotter or colder, just let me know," Beltine urged, drawing his *amina*'s attention. "I'll be happy to change it for you."

Kavan smiled up at him. "Thank you . . . for everything."

Winking, Beltine quipped, "Say that later after I'm done washing every inch of your body."

His nostrils flared, and heat entered Kavan's eyes. He opened his mouth, only to be interrupted by two sharp knocks coming from the outer door.

Grinning, Beltine ordered, "Hold that thought."

Beltine hurried back up the steps. After exiting the bathing chamber, he hustled to the front door. He checked over his shoulder, making certain no one could see into the other room, before he opened the door.

Huh. Just as Garnelle had warned, I'm protective of my amina's nudity.

Considering Kavan was a shifter and would be naked before and after shifting, Beltine made a mental note to get a handle on that. He didn't want to end up upset over nothing. From what Beltine understood, shifters weren't shy creatures.

That may work out well because I love the central baths. I bet Kavan will enjoy it also.

With that thought in mind, Beltine grabbed the cart of food Consifen had prepared and wheeled it into his suite.

CHAPTER SIX

Kavan breathed deeply as he waited for Beltine to return. Sweeping his gaze over the room, he marveled at the smooth stone beneath him, the deep basin around him, and the expanse of the room itself. Of course, Kavan figured it had something to do with the huge wingspan Beltine sported.

He needs more room.

Sliding his eyes closed, Kavan listened to what was going on in the next room. He stretched out his legs and enjoyed the heat slowly rising along his limbs. At the same time, he heard the clink of dishes and wondered what Beltine was doing out there.

A second later, Kavan had his answer.

Beltine appeared in the doorway, pushing a small, three-tiered trolley before him. There were dishes on the bottom and middle with a couple of carafes and cups on top. He spotted potatoes cooked several different ways as well as a couple of types of meat. There were noodle dishes, too.

Kavan's mouth watered in anticipation, and he sat up in his seat.

Obviously spotting the move, Beltine paused and held up his hand, staying the move. "I'll bring the trolley around," he told him. "I'll make us up some plates, and we can eat in the bath." Winking, Beltine added, "Just like I promised."

More than on board with that, Kavan nodded. He figured he should let the demon know that he was perfectly fine to stand now. He'd just needed a few minutes of recovery after his epic double orgasm, which had chased away the last of the pain from his shift that had been too-long denied.

Still, Kavan couldn't resist accepting a little pampering. Having seen his mother so happy when his father had taken the time to do something special, he finally understood. It wasn't what the activity was, but rather, it was the fact that a lover did it at all.

Kavan felt so very blessed that he'd been gifted with parents who were fated mates. Their alpha had urged their people to mate early and produce plenty of kids. Part of Kavan understood, since their herd had been small and there were only two other giraffe shifter herds within a day's drive. Their kind were rare, and their alpha had encouraged them to propagate so they didn't die out.

Still, between being bisexual and having a fated pairing as parents, Kavan had resisted his alpha's urgings. He'd wanted what his parents had always had.

And now, I do . . . or I will, once we finish bonding.

"Anything on here calling your name, my *amina*?" Beltine asked as he poured a pale-pink fluid into a glass. Holding it out to him, he urged, "Try this. I believe you'd call it a type of juice similar to a cross between orange and apple juice."

While slightly skeptical, Kavan took it. Before bringing it to his lips, he admitted, "I'd love to try everything. It all smells amazing."

Beltine grinned as he grabbed an empty plate. Then he began heaping food onto it. "Shifters have larger appetites, if I remember," he commented while adding several meat pieces that looked like baked chicken legs. "There's plenty more where this came from."

Kavan nodded even as his mouth watered. Sniffing the juice, he wasn't certain what he was smelling. There was a tang that reminded him of orange juice coupled with something sweet, like watermelon.

Taking a tentative sip, Kavan rolled the fluid across his tongue. It tasted similar to what he'd scented, except maybe with a dash of apple juice tossed in, too. Kavan took a larger sip, enjoying it.

Hell, it's the best juice I've had in decades.

Chuckling under his breath at his thoughts—*it's the only juice I've had in decades*—Kavan turned his attention to Beltine. Gasping, he nearly choked on the juice. His sexy demon had stripped out of his leather leggings and stood in all his naked glory—and there was a lot of glory.

Kavan had grown used to seeing Beltine walk around topless. After all, the demon had wings. He figured dealing with a shirt with the appendages would be a pain in the butt.

Now, every inch of Beltine's tall, strong frame was on clear display. His pale skin gleamed in the bathing room's bright lights. His white-blond hair hung around his shoulders in thick waves. Even his ice-blue eyes drew Kavan in, and he wanted to stare into their swirling depths to see if they held the mysteries of the universe.

As Beltine carried their plates over to the steps, Kavan practically drooled over the movement of his strong thighs and sexy ass-cheeks. The demon turned, revealing a half-hard cock and a hairless groin. Kavan had to swallow hard to keep from allowing that drool to dribble down his chin.

"Holy shit," Kavan whispered, unable to help himself. Snapping his focus up to his demon's face—*and he is all mine*—Kavan took in the male's pleased expression. "You're stunning, but I bet you knew that."

Beltine shrugged as he stepped into the water. "I know I think you're sexy and have heard that it's part of the pull to mate or bond or whatever any paranormal group calls it." Setting a plate down on either side of Kavan's shoulders, Beltine placed his knuckles on the stone next to him and leaned in close. "As long as you're attracted to me, I couldn't give a shit what reason someone puts behind it."

Then Beltine began to lean in, and Kavan knew the male planned to kiss him.

As much as Kavan wanted that, too, he turned his head.

Beltine growled, his displeasure clear. "What do you think you're doing, Kavan?"

"I need to brush my teeth," Kavan told him. "I can't even guess at how long it's been."

Grunting in annoyance, Beltine pulled away. Instead of sitting beside him, he strode purposefully from the sunken tub. He climbed out and crossed to a wicker cabinet against one wall. After fishing around inside it, Beltine returned.

Holding up a hand, Beltine revealed what he'd retrieved — a toothbrush and a tube.

Kavan assumed it contained some kind of tooth-cleaning agent.

"Brush your teeth, my *amina*," Beltine grumbled, pointing at the still pouring faucet. "I don't wish to be denied again."

Taking the offered items, Kavan stated solemnly, "I'm not denying you, Beltine." He poured the fluid — which looked more like a purple ointment — onto the brush. "Please understand, I've been in my giraffe form for decades. I just . . . wanted to clean my mouth."

Hell, it was a good idea to do that before and after eating, too.

Rubbing the back of his neck, Beltine grimaced. "My apologies for my annoyance. Your action surprised me, and I — " He shook his head before forcing a smile. "It's not something I've ever processed before. I reacted badly."

Slipping to his knees, Kavan began knee-walking toward the pouring water. "We all have things we'll have to get used to. A relationship is new to me, too." He stopped before it and cocked his head. "You want me to just spit into the water?"

Beltine pointed at the rock lining the wall at the deepest end of the pool. "That's a filter. If you try, you'll feel the circulation of the water. The water is constantly being cleaned." Shrugging, he added, "While bubble baths are pretty much out, the other filter on the shallow end adds in minerals to aid in muscle and skin regeneration."

Nodding slowly, Kavan began brushing his teeth. As he processed that, something occurred to him. "It's kinda like a dip in a mineral hot springs."

Arching a brow, Beltine quirked up the left side of his mouth. "I'll take your word for it."

Kavan snickered around his toothbrush. He scrubbed quickly, wanting to be finished. The ointment tasted surprisingly similar to the juice.

After finishing, Kavan set both items aside before cupping his hands and beginning to rinse his mouth. To his surprise, he saw Beltine grab the items and reapply the ointment. Then the demon began brushing his own teeth.

Okay.

While Kavan had never shared a toothbrush in his life, it was obvious that the demon didn't think anything of it. Perhaps it was a mate thing. Then it occurred to Kavan that the problem might lie with him.

I'm about to share the rest of my body with this male, why not my mouth? After all, I plan to suck his dick at some point.

Yep. It's definitely me.

Easing back to his seat, Kavan waited, ignoring his grumbling stomach and the delicious aroma of fresh food.

Kiss first. Food later.

Kavan watched Beltine spit in the direction of the filter. Then he swished the toothbrush under the water before setting it aside. Bending, Beltine held his head under the faucet with his mouth open for an instant before closing it, then spitting.

With his fingers twitching with his desire to brush those wet strands away from Beltine's high-cheekboned-features, Kavan licked his lips. He watched the demon do that a second time before his patience came to an end. Leaning forward, Kavan grabbed Beltine around the waist and jerked the male toward him.

Beltine's expression held one of surprise, but he didn't fight Kavan, for which he was grateful.

Kavan relaxed back in his seat, Beltine cradled between his thighs. Threading one hand in the demon's white wet hair, he cradled his nape with the other. He used the hold to urge Beltine's mouth to his own.

To Kavan's delight, Beltine immediately opened for him, so he thrust his tongue inside. He swished it inside the other male, enjoying his slightly salty masculine flavor, even just a bit hidden by the demon-style toothpaste. Taking his time, Kavan tangled his tongue with Beltine's, mapping his mouth and enjoying the simple pleasure of it with no rush to move on to more carnal pursuits.

Kavan's stomach rumbled once more, loud enough to be heard over the sound of the flowing water.

Beltine drew back, a grin showing off his sharp teeth. "I think it's time to feed you, my *amina*."

Before allowing his demon to draw away, Kavan told him, "I apologize for turning away from you. I didn't mean it the way you took it."

Smiling, Beltine rubbed a thumb over Kavan's brow fondly. "I know, Kavan. I know." Lifting one shoulder in a half-shrug, he admitted, "I took it poorly, not understanding." After pecking Kavan's lips in another quick kiss, Beltine stated confidently, "We'll find our footing in this relationship of ours. You did just turn human, you know."

Nodding, Kavan relaxed back in his seat.

Settling in a curve of rock directly to his right, Beltine spread his legs enough so their knees bumped under the water. "Here." He leaned over Kavan, rubbing his torso against Kavan's provocatively as he grabbed the plate on the other side of him. Straightening, Beltine held the plate out to him.

"If you don't like something, please don't feel as if you have to eat it. And if you do like something, don't hesitate to ask for seconds." Then Beltine winked. "And don't forget to save room for dessert."

Chuckling softly, Kavan took the plate and peered over the offerings, quickly deciding what to try first. It all looked fantastic.

"Oh, one more thing."

Kavan turned his attention on Beltine and saw that he was holding out a thick reed mat. Before Beltine, a similar mat was floating in the water. The demon's plate rested upon it.

"Nice." Kavan took the mat and mirrored Beltine's set-up.

Then Kavan grabbed the thing that looked like baked chicken and dug in.

CHAPTER SEVEN

Beltine watched with pleasure as his *amina* ate heartily. Kavan hummed and nodded, smiled at him, and licked his fingers. After eating all three pieces of game hen breasts, he hesitated. Then he snagged a potato wedge. They'd been baked in bacon grease and shredded leeks with a sprinkling of garlic.

In Beltine's opinion, they were damn fantastic.

After a second, Kavan popped the food into his mouth. He chewed twice before pausing. Then his eyes lit up, and he groaned.

"Oh, gods," Kavan mumbled around his mouthful of food. "So good."

Chuckling, Beltine nodded, grabbing a wedge of his own. While chewing, he recalled something unexpected he'd spotted on the tray. Evidently, Consifen had remembered that Kavan was from the human plane—the same place as Master Famine's lovers.

And they like to use silverware instead of a knife or their claws.

Beltine leaned toward the tray and grabbed the fork he'd found. Settling back in his seat, he held it out to his lover.

Kavan paused with another wedge halfway to his lips. Spotting the utensil, he grinned and took it. Then he popped the wedge into his mouth before using the fork to scoop up a heaping amount of scrambled game hen eggs mixed with diced peppers and leeks.

When Kavan shoved the forkful into his mouth, he managed to chew twice before his eyes widened. His nostrils flared, and his cheeks flushed a deep pink. He dropped his fork onto his plate. Then he grabbed his glass of juice from the side of the bath and took a huge gulp.

Realizing his mistake, Beltine touched his *amina's* shoulder. "I'm so sorry, Kavan. I should have said something." He watched his shifter take another swig of juice as he said, "Those little blue bits in there are peppers . . . and some find them pretty spicy."

"Some?" Kavan gasped, clearly struggling with the heat.

Beltine nodded. "Some demons do, some don't." With a depreciative smile, he admitted, "I don't, so I totally forgot when I piled them on your plate. My apologies."

Blowing out a breath, Kavan held up his glass. "It's okay, and if you have more juice over there, I forgive you."

Chuckling with relief, Beltine nodded. "Thank you." He stood and grabbed the carafe off the top of the trolley. "And of course." After refilling his *amina's* glass, Beltine settled back in his seat as he placed the carafe off to the side. "I'm glad you like the juice. It's the only kind we make in the demon realm." He pointed at a slice of fruit that, if he were human, would think looked like a peach. "We call that a Pimona. It's where the juice comes from. It'll help cool your tongue."

Kavan took Beltine at his word. He grabbed a slice and shoved it into his mouth. Instantly, he relaxed against his seat, sighing softly as he chewed. After swallowing so hard his Adam's apple bobbed, Kavan took a second piece.

"Try the bacon," Beltine encouraged next. "It's salted in a maple brine, then smoked for almost a day in our kitchen's outdoor smokehouse." Shaking his head, Beltine grumbled, "Those guys get out of many assignments due to their skills, but gods, is it worth it to the rest of us."

Picking up the indicated piece of meat, Kavan asked, "So, you explained how each of you are created by the gods, then assigned to one of the horseman, whom you're bonded with in lieu of a soul."

Nodding, Beltine waited for the actual question as he popped his own piece of pork into his mouth.

"Well, how does it work when you go to my plane?" Kavan cocked his head with his eyes narrowed. "I imagine Famine doesn't go with many of you on assignments."

"Oh." Beltine understood. "We're still connected to him, but it's through the task we have to do. Our job is to create famine in locations, which is normally caused by lack of rainfall, but there can be other reasons, too." He paused, sorting through his explanation. "For example, a flood can cause famine, so maybe I accomplish this by using my skills to create excessive amounts of rainfall in the mountains, resulting in flash floods, which wipe out crops downstream."

The more Beltine spoke, the wider Kavan's jaw sagged open. Still, it was his job, so he continued to attempt to explain. "I'm connected with your birth plane by the task I'm assigned. Once the job is done, my grip on your plane wanes, eventually forcing me back to this one. The older I am, the longer I can resist the pull, should I choose." Shrugging, Beltine admitted, "There's very little reason for me to do that, though, since even to have sex, I'm using magick to hide my true self from whoever I'm fucking."

In truth, staying in the human realm was more trouble than it was worth, in Beltine's opinion.

Kavan's concerned expression warped into a snarl so swiftly it took Beltine's breath away. His shifter pushed into his space. Gripping his thigh in one hand, Kavan snagged his wrist with the other.

"You're *mine*, Beltine," Kavan declared. "No one else's. You got it?" His fingers tightened, although not enough to cause pain. "Tell me you got it."

Beltine felt his breathing hitch in his chest upon taking in Kavan's possessiveness. "I got it," he quickly whispered, his blood heating in his veins. Seeing Kavan's eyes narrow as he swept his gaze over his face, Beltine realized his *amina* was checking to make certain he'd gotten the message. Beltine smiled as he rubbed a forefinger down Kavan's neck, lightly touching the mark he'd left there. "I'm all yours," he assured. "Just like you're all mine."

Kavan's jaw flexed as he relaxed back in his seat. "I want to mark you," he stated bluntly even as he released him. Turning his attention to his food, Kavan picked up another potato wedge. "I hope you don't have any plans for after our bath and meal other than fucking me face to face so I can mark your neck."

It was Beltine's turn to nearly choke on the piece of game hen he'd just popped into his mouth.

Smirking, Kavan handed him his glass of juice.

Beltine gratefully took it. After a couple of gulps, he managed to get himself under control. He set the glass on the side of the bathing pool before returning his focus to Kavan.

"Okay. Yes. You're my priority right now," Beltine told his *amina*. Master Famine had been extremely understanding considering the oddness of their meeting. Knowing he had to be honest, Beltine told his shifter, "I don't know how long I can put off my duties now that you've shifted, but until Master Famine says otherwise, I'm here with you."

Kavan nodded, his brows furrowing. "I suppose that's the same with any paranormal group."

Stabbing a potato wedge with his foreclaw, Beltine asked, "What do you mean?"

Grimacing, Kavan told him, "There was this one time that my alpha ordered my father to be part of a tracking party." His expression turned pained. "They were being sent to find the trail of a herd-member, um, Pako, who'd chosen to leave because he found his fated mate in a human." Shaking his head, Kavan whispered, "Trying to stop a shifter from being with his fated mate went against everything my father believed in, but he'd been ordered to go."

Beltine watched as Kavan popped a piece of fruit into his mouth and chewed, his features a little vacant. It was clear that he was recalling the past. For a good moment, Beltine allowed his *amina* to drift.

Then Beltine decided it was time to draw Kavan out of his obviously distressing memory.

Touching Kavan's jaw, Beltine asked softly, "Do you want to tell me what happened?"

Kavan blinked once, then refocused on him. He smiled. "Oh, my father was blessed by the gods," he claimed with a quiet grunt. "He was sent with the group that went in the wrong direction." Smirking, Kavan told him, "The group that did track Pako missed him by fifteen minutes. The family of the man's mate whisked him away."

"That's fantastic," Beltine responded with a laugh. Then he had to know, "How did they know he was being followed?"

With a wry smile, Kavan told him, "From what I heard, Pako told his mate that he was trying to escape the mob, and his new family made it happen." He shrugged. "Other than a bus ticket out of town, the trackers never found anything."

"Damn. Very nice." Beltine grinned as he thought about the escaped shifter. Then he sobered. "Why did you tell me that tale?"

"Oh." Kavan laughed. "I just wanted you to know that if you're sent away, I'll understand that it's not because you want to leave my side, but it's because your alpha, uh, Master Famine, orders you to do so."

Beltine relaxed, feeling relieved that Kavan understood.

Then Kavan frowned at his plate as he muttered, "I'd really like to know what happened to my family." He lifted his head and met Beltine's gaze. "It wouldn't surprise me if our alpha refused to bother looking for me, considering I refused to breed for him, but I need to know my parents are okay."

Nodding, Beltine quickly thought about who could help with that. His thoughts immediately turned to Master Famine's bonded men, and he wondered if they would be willing to help. Perhaps he would approach Hank. The human was kind and friendly, and he seemed to be concerned with not only Famine but also with those demons under his command.

Hell, Beltine recalled the human spotting a demon—Diederan—with a broken arm and asking the male if he could help him with anything. Of course, Diederan had gaped at him as if he were a fish out of water. The youngster had obviously not known how to respond.

Garnelle had saved Diederan, assuring Hank that he would be well taken care of. It was true, too. Demons took care of their own. Sure, in the training ring, the trainers would beat the crap out of those they trained, but it was all in the name of getting them strong enough to be safe on the human plane.

Sometimes, the human plane was not a nice place, especially for younger demons.

Beltine believed that humans' stories of demons were actually caused by a youngster losing control of their magick. The havoc or problems that they could cause were hard to cover up. Humans loved to share tall tales, often making them even wilder and grander with each retelling.

What most people called fish tales.

"I'll need some more information about your prior herd," Beltine began slowly. "Location as well as who the alpha was." He smiled encouragingly as he added, "Your parents' names. Other family. And I'll see what can be found out about them."

Kavan nodded. "I'll give you everything you need." Then he picked up his reed mat, the plate with it, and set it on the side of the bathing pool. "But right now"—Kavan turned and slid closer to Beltine—"are you done with breakfast?"

Beltine instantly scented Kavan's arousal. His nostrils flared as he inhaled the delicious goodness signifying his shifter's need. With his cock swiftly taking notice, Beltine moved his own mat out of the way, then reached for Kavan.

"I—" Before Beltine could say more, a hard knock sounded on his door. Frowning, he groaned. "There can be few who that could be." Beltine offered Kavan a heartfelt expression of regret. "I'll try to get rid of them as swiftly as possible, then return."

Even as Kavan nodded, Beltine could scent his disappointment.

Still, as his shifter had indicated, the male understood duty.

Beltine hurried from the bathing chamber, grabbing a towel on his way. He'd just managed to wrap it around his waist when the knock came again. Lifting his hand while scowling, Beltine prepared to holler at whoever was being such a demanding, forceful asshole.

"Try to relax, my shifter. He could be in the middle of something."

Recognizing Master Famine's voice, Beltine froze. He closed his eyes for a heartbeat and did his best to get his arousal under control, realizing that fucking was off the table for who knew how long. Then Beltine opened his eyes and the door.

"Master Famine," Beltine greeted, dipping his head in greeting. "I'm honored."

Beltine was telling the truth. Any time their horseman took time to visit them, regardless of the reason, it truly was an honor.

Sweeping his gaze over Beltine, Famine offered him the smallest of smiles. "I do apologize for interrupting, my demon, but I must speak with you . . . and you should probably have your *amina* at your side."

Beltine nodded. "Of course. I'll get him."

Famine stepped into the room followed by his shifter, Knossis, who had evidently been the one knocking.

"We'll gather drinks in your kitchen," Famine stated.

Nodding, Beltine recognized what his master was doing — giving him time to go to his bedchambers to dress.

He plans to be here for a few minutes, at least.

CHAPTER EIGHT

Having recognized Famine's voice, Kavan had been out of the tub and already drying off. When he'd followed Beltine into the bedroom, who was whispering his apologies, he'd waved away his concern. Hell, a herd-member would never turn their alpha away at their door, no matter the reason.

Once in the bedroom, Kavan appreciated that Beltine's cotton linen pants — ones he said he sometimes slept in — fit him once he cinched the tie tight around his slender hips.

Moments later, Kavan found himself seated beside Beltine on one of his plush, ottoman-style sofas. Hank, Famine's human lover, served them drinks under the watchful eye of Knossis. Of course, the big shifter seemed to watch everything like a hawk.

Chissom and Famine waited on another, slightly larger sofa. Once drinks were served, Hank sat partly on the vampire's lap as well as Famine's while Knossis squeezed onto the end. Famine was definitely squished in the middle.

Still, Kavan thought Famine appeared extremely pleased with their positioning.

Huh.

Holding his drink with one hand, Kavan leaned into Beltine's side, and his demon wrapped not only an arm but a wing around him, tucking him close. He focused on Famine and realized the horseman was staring at his neck — or more specifically, the mark Beltine had left upon it. His scrutiny caused a fissure of nerves to trickle up his spine.

Famine's attention flicked to Kavan's face, and a small smile lifted the corners of his mouth. "Let's start with the elephant in the room. Shall we?"

"Of course, Master Famine," Beltine replied respectfully.

"The early meeting of your *amina*." As Beltine nodded, Famine focused on Kavan. "Did Beltine explain all that to you?"

Kavan nodded. "Yes, Master Famine. He hasn't completed a thousand years of service, yet."

"Correct, which means he does not have the magick built within him, yet, to complete the soul-tearing ritual." Famine tipped his head to the side as his eyes narrowed a little. "There is a way around it, but—"

Knossis growled low in his throat, clearly not pleased with what Famine was about to say.

Famine looked his lover's way. Lifting his arm, he rested his palm on the shifter's neck. "Easy, my chosen," he murmured. "Would you have liked to have waited over two decades to claim us?"

After grumbling under his breath for a few seconds, Knossis grudgingly admitted, "No."

"Well, then."

Even as Famine began again, Chissom and Hank exchanged an uneasy glance.

Famine must have noticed, for he pressed a quick kiss to Hank's temple as he threaded the fingers of his other hand through Chissom's sandy-brown hair.

Returning his focus to them, Famine finally finished his earlier thought. "But it is dangerous . . . and probably extremely painful for Kavan. As you know, the fourth session of the soul-tearing ritual must be completed in the human realm." Famine glanced between them, but when neither of them said anything, he continued. "My belief that it is painful for you, Kavan, is because there will only be *one* session of soul-tearing as opposed to spreading it out over four times. My belief that it is dangerous stems from the fact that it will take the combined powers of myself and my three brothers . . . which would leave us vulnerable."

"And if any of our enemies were to find out," Knossis snarled, his eyes narrowing. He even cracked his knuckles as if anticipating a beat-down to whoever might possibly betray them.

"I vow that no one will hear of it from me," Beltine quickly claimed. Using his free hand to cup Kavan's jaw, he drew his attention. "What of you, my *amina*? I hear the soul-tearing is painful as it is. To have to endure the agony of four sessions in one?" Beltine grimaced. "That would be pure torture for you. I'm not certain it's worth it. Perhaps we should be patient."

Nuzzling into Beltine's grip, Kavan rested his palm on his demon's chest. "I'm not concerned about me," he stated, searching his mate's expression. "I'm worried about you. I'd be willing to accept any agony to share my life properly with you, but I know you hate the idea of harming me . . . even a little."

Even if Kavan hadn't been certain before, just the fact that Beltine was willing to wait over two decades was a dead giveaway.

Beltine inhaled deeply, his eyes closing. After a heartbeat, he let it back out slowly and refocused on Kavan. "You've already been through so much, but I told you once that I'd never take away your right to choose."

"What about *your* right to choose?" Kavan countered. "I won't force you to do something you don't want to do."

His features twisting into a grimace, Beltine whispered, "I want to do this so fucking badly." He followed his admittance by adding, "And I feel like the most selfish asshole in history for it because I know it'll hurt you."

Kavan chuckled softly as he rubbed up and down Beltine's torso, enjoying the feel of the hard flesh beneath his palm. "Then we both want the same thing." As Kavan held Beltine's gaze, he nodded once, slowly. "Right?"

Beltine pinned him with a searching look, then returned Kavan's nod. "Right."

Turning his attention back to Famine, Kavan smiled tightly. "We would be honored if you and your brothers were to perform the ritual."

"There is one other thing I forgot to mention," Famine added, his attention straying left and right to his lovers.

Knossis crossed his brawny arms over his torso and glared at them. "You'll have an audience," the shifter stated gruffly. His tone just dared them to deny him.

"Uh, an audience?" Beltine questioned. "What kind of audience? Who? Why?"

"Well, obviously myself and my brothers," Famine began, stating what should have been obvious. "Since we're performing the ritual, but we'll keep our backs to you."

"*I'll* be there," Knossis declared. "And I *won't* be keeping my back to you." Even as Beltine opened his mouth, the big shifter stated, "I can't keep watch over my lover if I'm only looking in one direction."

Kavan could understand that. Even as his animal bellowed in his mind about how no one should see their mate in the throes of ecstasy but him, he did his best to shush that side of himself. He mentally reminded his giraffe that they both wanted the same thing, and this was the only way to get it . . . unless they wanted to wait.

His inner giraffe quieted after a few more grumbles, accepting the inevitable.

"I'll be there as well," Chissom announced.

Hank narrowed his eyes before stating, "As will I." All three of his men opened their mouths, but the cute human lifted his hand — and his voice — as he added, "No way are my men going to a ritual bonding ceremony without me." Hank's eyes narrowed as he stared each man down, saying, "Ritual bonding means sex. Sex means pheromones. That means you all will end up wanting to have sex, too, once it's complete, so" — he crossed his arms over his torso and tipped his chin up haughtily — "I will be there."

Famine, Chissom, and Knossis began glancing between each other.

Beltine had told Kavan how the foursome had ended up with a mind-link — probably a byproduct from bonding with a vampire and a horseman. He would bet his bottom dollar — if he had one — that they were having a swift and private conversation between them.

Even as Kavan wondered if he would end up having a link with Beltine, Hank growled softly and snapped, "It's not nice to talk behind someone's back."

Evidently, their human had figured it out, too.

"Sorry, babe," Chissom immediately purred into Hank's ear, rubbing a palm up and down his back. "We don't mean to upset you."

"And, yet, you do," Hank grumped, scowling at them all. "Don't treat me like glass just because I'm human. I get that I'm not a fighter, and I would never seek it out, but you're my men, and I want" — he paused and shook his head — "I *need* to be there with you."

Famine skimmed the backs of his fingertips along Hank's jaw. "Yes, my chosen human. Of course, we want you there."

"We always want you with us," Knossis rumbled, still appearing concerned. His expression screamed that he wished he could come up with something to convince Hank to stay home. "We just want you safe, too."

"So I'll pick up my gun from the coven house, first," Hank told them with a shrug. "Master Dante moved it to the gun safe in the study when I cleaned out my room."

All three men stared at Hank in obvious surprise.

Chissom was the first to gather himself. "How come I never knew you had a gun, let alone know how to use it?"

During one of Beltine's many rambles while Kavan had still been in animal form, his demon had explained that Hank had originally been a donor for Chissom's vampire coven.

Hank snorted as he smirked at Chissom. "No offense, but when we got together over the years, gun-talk was definitely nowhere near what you had in mind." While Chissom chuckled, his gaze turning heated as he smirked at Hank, the human winked and continued, "Ruth and Second Kellan taught me."

Kavan sifted through names quickly.

Ah, Ruth is Master Dante's beloved. Right.

The title of Second before Kellan's name made recalling who he was easy enough.

"Well, it's settled then," Famine murmured, smiling. "We'll pick up your gun first."

While nodding his agreement, Knossis stated, "And I think we should take two dozen demons . . . just in case."

Famine sighed deeply, but he nodded once more. "I have a funny feeling each of my brothers are going to be doing this exact same thing," he admitted. Shaking his head, he wondered, "Where the hell are we going to find a large enough and secluded enough place to actually hold this ceremony?"

"The ranch," Chissom replied confidently. "The coven has plenty of acreage, some of it pretty remote. Master Dante will allow us to use a spot there."

"It could bring danger to his ranch and coven," Famine countered, not sounding as if he agreed.

Scoffing, Chissom reminded everyone, "There's already danger to our ranch and coven."

"But more?" Famine pressed.

Chissom smiled indulgently at the horseman, which was

something Kavan would never have expected anyone to do, let alone that Famine would tolerate it.

Leaning over, Chissom pecked a kiss to Famine's pale lips. "Then we'll just have to ask him."

Famine nodded. "Yes, we shall." His voice had lowered, turning husky, and his gaze fell to Chissom's lips when the vampire began to straighten.

From the rising pheromones in the room, Kavan could guess where Famine's attention was straying to.

Beltine obviously figured it out, too, for he cleared his throat before saying, "Uh, while that's sorted, may I have permission to track down Kavan's parents? He'd like to check on them."

Knossis tore his focus away from his lovers. "We've already found them." The broad shifter pointed at Kavan. "For the record, I think your alpha's an asshole."

Kavan gaped. While he never would have said it out loud, he did agree with the fox shifter. Alpha Anthony was indeed an asshole.

"How did you find them already?" Beltine asked what Kavan was wondering.

"I ran into Consifen in the dining hall," Hank told them. While his face was flushed and he shifted on the laps of his men, he focused on Kavan. "He was super excited and told us that you'd finally shifted. He also gave us your name."

"Hank told me," Chissom cut in. "And I was able to cross-reference your name against a list of known missing shifters that my coven received from the Vampire Council, which they'd received from the Shifter Council." He pointed at Kavan. "You were reported missing by your parents twelve years ago, but when a shifter council enforcer questioned your ex-alpha to try to follow up on your disappearance, Anthony claimed you'd run off and your parents just didn't want to accept it." Sneering, Chissom added, "If you want us to help you relocate your parents to a nicer herd, just say the word."

Gaping, Kavan nodded as his mind reeled. "Wow. Okay. Yeah, my alpha really *is* an asshole."

"*Ex*-alpha," Beltine corrected on a grumble, holding him tight. "You're not his anymore."

Kavan nodded again, more than happy with that.

CHAPTER NINE

The next morning, the group headed to Master Dante's coven. The vampire master greeted them warmly and congratulated them on finding each other. His beloved offered them refreshments to enjoy while waiting for their call with Councilman Nigel Granis — a Siberian tiger shifter — which Second Kellan had set up for them.

Beltine and Kavan were shown to a large study by Kellan, while the others headed elsewhere with Master Dante. He knew Famine and his men intended to discuss a location for the ritual. As he sipped a cup of hot chocolate — Kavan choosing black tea — they watched a young human named Raphael check settings and cables on a large monitor and computer.

While Beltine would be the first to admit he wasn't very well versed in technology, Raphael seemed to know exactly what he was doing.

Right on time, a call came in from a shifter named Karnak, calling on behalf of Councilman Nigel Granis. Raphael accepted the call and introduced Beltine and Kavan before excusing himself. In seconds, they were talking to a Shifter Councilman.

After conversing with Nigel, it had been decided that they would arrive at Alpha Anthony's herd unannounced. They would be accompanied by a pair of Shifter Council Enforcers — a komodo dragon shifter named Dane Drudeson as well as a water buffalo shifter named Austin O'Malley. When the shifters appeared on screen, they both seemed to be the big dominant sort, which Beltine guessed was typical of shifter council enforcers.

Beltine was pleased to find that they were sympathetic and understanding even as they congratulated them on finding their fated mate. Unable to help himself, Beltine lifted his hand to Kavan's claiming scar. The sex they'd shared the evening before, after Famine and his men had left their suite, had been the best of Beltine's life.

For the first time in Beltine's nearly thousand-year-long life, he'd experienced his *lackchet* – or sucker's hook. After pouring his release into Kavan's hot, tight chute, the extension to his penis had eased from his slit and attached to his *amina*'s prostate. As micro-orgasms had burst through Beltine's body, the stimulation to his lover had nearly caused Kavan's eyes to roll to the back of his head.

When Kavan had sunk his canines into Beltine's neck, claiming him in the shifter way, they'd both passed out.

Just thinking about it caused Beltine's blood to flow south and his balls to tingle. He could hardly wait to experience that again. Unfortunately, they'd slept too late that morning and had to satisfy themselves with quick hand jobs in the shower, although even that had been nearly mind-bending.

"I can tell what you're thinking about," Kavan whispered into his ear. "Settle down unless you want me to take you into the bathroom of this backroad diner and have my way with you."

Beltine groaned even as he pinned a feral stare on Kavan. "You're not helping." A glance at the clock over the diner's door told him they didn't have time. "Dane and Austin should be here any second."

Beltine had zipped himself and Kavan along a lei line, placing them about an hour south of Alpha Anthony's herd lands.

As if conjured by Beltine's comment, the pair of enforcers walked into the diner. It was easy to see that both men were nearly as tall as him – maybe off by an inch – but they were damn broad and heavily muscled. As they made their way to Beltine and Kavan's table, every pair of eyes in the place turned in their direction.

Rising to his feet, Beltine offered his hand. Dane took it first. "It's good to meet you. Thank you for coming."

Dane swept his gaze over him once, twice, before saying, "Same to you." He used the thumb of his free hand to indicate Kavan, who was in the process of greeting Austin. "I recognize Kavan but wasn't certain about you. Beltine, isn't it?"

Beltine grinned and nodded, understanding Dane's confusion. On the video call, he'd been in his true form. Before arriving at the diner, he'd cast a glamour spell. Anyone other than his *amina* would see a muscular, six-foot-six guy, with lightly tanned skin and blond hair.

"Sorry for the confusion." Beltine eased back into his chair, Kavan doing the same. Tipping his chin toward the approaching waiter—a human probably in the early twenty range—Beltine lowered his voice and murmured, "I apologize for not warning you."

Waving away his apology, Dane smirked. "Naw. Don't worry about it." Then he turned a charming smile upon the human, and the sweet scent of arousal instantly perfumed the air. "Hello, cutie," Dane greeted confidently. "How about a cup of coffee? And how are your pancakes?"

"O-Our pancakes are e-excellent, sir," the waiter murmured, his voice squeaking just a little as he peered through his lashes at the massive blond. "As are the sausage links."

Beltine relaxed in his seat and slung his arm over the back of Kavan's chair.

"We're not in a hurry, are we?" Dane asked, sweeping his gaze around at everyone.

Austin focused on his menu as he rumbled, "Nope. Take your time, Dane. We got all morning."

"Excellent." Dane pinned a look on their waiter that could

only be called eye-fucking, causing the human to flush to the roots of his hair. "I'll take your farmer's platter and upgrade that to all-you-can-eat pancakes."

From looking at the menu earlier—although they'd only ordered drinks, hot chocolate and tea again—Beltine knew that meal included bacon, sausage, ham, two eggs, grits, biscuits and gravy, baked apples, and the persons' choice of pancakes, waffles, or French toast.

Seems trying to pick up a fuck makes the komodo dragon shifter hungry.

"A-And how would you like your eggs?" the waiter asked. While he was probably going for sultry, it didn't quite work.

Dane didn't seem to mind. "Over-easy"—he glanced pointedly at the young male's nametag—"Danny."

The waiter—Danny—tried to hide it, but he trembled for an instant. "A-And to d-drink?"

"Coffee," Dane replied, not seeming to mind that he had to repeat himself. "Danny."

Ah, the poor kid. No idea what he's getting himself into.

Danny nodded, then turned. He'd taken two steps before realizing there were still other people at the table. Turning back, he cleared his throat. Danny seemed incapable of making eye-contact with any of them as he took their orders.

As Danny moved away from their table, Dane watched him go . . . and none-too-covertly.

"Well, hell," Austin rumbled as he turned his attention to Dane. Pushing his shaggy, dark hair from his eyes, he cocked his head. "Never heard of you fuckin' around on assignment before."

Dane just smirked as he relaxed in his chair, since Danny had disappeared into the kitchen.

"Um, you may want to tone it down a little," Kavan murmured, scratching his finger over the scuffed wood of the table. "The hostess is scowling in the direction Danny disappeared."

Growling under his breath, Dane nodded once. "Thanks. Don't wanna get him in trouble."

A few minutes later, Danny returned with their drinks — coffees for the enforcers and refills for Beltine and Kavan. While Austin rumbled a thanks, Dane just winked at him and slid a napkin toward him. After a second of hesitation, Danny slid it off the table and shoved it into his pocket.

"Dare I ask?" Austin muttered.

Dane smiled at his friend. "How about you go distract the hostess for a few minutes for me?"

Austin scowled and lowered his voice. "How the hell do you expect me to do that?"

"I'll do it," Beltine offered, rising from his seat. As a demon, it would be a snap. Plus, he wanted to see if Dane actually managed to score. With a wink at Kavan, Beltine stated, "Take as much time as you need."

Grinning broadly, Dane replied, "Good man."

Beltine headed to the front, hearing Austin hiss, "You are such a hound, Dane."

"Not really," Dane countered, but if he said anything else, Beltine missed it over the sounds of the diner.

Reaching the front, Beltine caught the woman's attention. As soon as her gaze met his own, he eased into her mind. Beltine immediately discovered that she didn't like Danny because he was gay and because he was the son of the town alcoholic.

Beltine couldn't do anything about either one, but he could do as he'd said — distract her for a few minutes.

"Is everything okay?" Peggy asked.

Smiling, Beltine replied, "Indeed it is. Our waiter is doing a marvelous job." Then he spent nearly ten minutes chatting with her in an inane conversation about their hot chocolate.

Beltine noticed Dane slip into the bathroom. Danny joined him a few seconds later. They were in there for a good six minutes before Danny left first, looking flushed and more than a little rumpled. Beltine hoped he stopped at the break-room to straighten up first.

Dane returned to their table, his lips curved in a smile that looked equal parts smug and satisfied.

Huh. Go Dane.

With a little push into Peggy's mind, Beltine confirmed that she hadn't seen a thing. He also removed her memory of Dane flirting with Danny before implanting the idea that the waiter was nothing but the model employee. As Beltine closed out his conversation with Peggy, he hoped that would keep her off his back at work . . . at least, for a little while.

Returning to the table, Beltine scented the unmistakable aroma of sex. What surprised him was that Dane continued to smell of arousal. Evidently, Danny must have been good because Dane wanted him again.

Odd.

Beltine settled back in his seat and quirked an eyebrow at Dane.

The komodo dragon shifter appeared relaxed, but for some reason, Beltine could see a hint of tension around his eyes, even when Dane smiled at him.

"Is everything okay?" Beltine asked as he settled his hand over Kavan's thigh.

Dane nodded. "Yup. Never better."

Before Beltine could think of a way to pry, Danny arrived carrying a large platter laden with food. It was so big that he nearly bobbled the thing as he set it on a nearby empty table. Dane instantly gripped the edge, steadying it and saving their waiter from making a big mess.

Danny smiled shyly at Dane, whispering a thank you.

After Danny had placed their spread before them, they all tucked into their food. As was pretty standard with four hungry men, not much was said for a good fifteen minutes — well, other than pass the syrup. Danny returned to top off the enforcers' coffees, but Beltine declined a third hot chocolate. Kavan asked for a water, which Danny swiftly supplied.

When Danny brought the bill, Dane snatched it, insisting on paying for everyone. As they all rose, the komodo dragon shifter pulled out his wallet and fished through it. He laid several folded bills on the table along with the ticket.

Beltine knew he wasn't the best at judging human money, but he was pretty damn sure their meal hadn't cost anywhere close to a hundred dollars, and that was just the bill Beltine could see.

Austin led the way to a rented SUV and climbed behind the wheel.

Dane settled in the passenger seat.

Climbing in the back, Beltine relaxed with his arm around Kavan's shoulders.

"Anything you wanna talk about?" Austin asked Dane as he brought the vehicle roaring to life.

Grinning at Austin, Dane quipped, "Nope."

Beltine didn't know the shifter, so he didn't feel it was his place to pry. Besides, he had more important things to focus on, namely, his tense *amina* beside him.

Squeezing Kavan against him, Beltine pecked a kiss to his temple.

"All will be well, my *amina*."

Kavan smiled back, the expression tight. "I hope so."

Chapter Ten

Spotting Alpha Anthony's house in the distance, Kavan felt his stomach twist. The food he'd eaten sat like a lead weight within him. Clenching and unclenching his hands, he tried to relieve the sudden tension.

"Try to relax, Kavan," Beltine crooned, nuzzling his nose against the claiming scar at his neck. "There's nothing he can do to you."

"What if he won't let me see my parents?" Kavan asked. Then he grimaced and expressed his greatest fear. "What if they don't want to see me?"

"Don't worry, Kavan," Dane assured, turning in his seat to peer at them. "They'll definitely want to see you, and the alpha can't keep you apart." With a rakish grin, he added, "And if he tries, we're well within our rights to remove your parents here and now."

Blowing out a breath, Kavan rubbed his palms over his cargo shorts. "Okay." He did his best to smile. "Thank you."

"We would have just gone straight to your parents," Austin stated, his deep voice flat. "But it's courtesy to present yourself to the alpha of the territory."

Kavan blew out a breath. He knew that, too.

"What happens if he tries to attack us?" The question was out of Kavan's mouth before he could think better of it.

Austin tipped his head up and looked at him through the rearview mirror. "Okay, why would you even think that's feasible?"

Shaking his head, Kavan tried to sort his crazy thoughts. "I don't know." He just as quickly tacked on, "Because we're about to prove that he lied? He doesn't like it when he doesn't get his way."

"We'll remain vigilant," Dane assured. "But let's worry about that if it happens. No sense in borrowing trouble."

Beltine squeezed his shoulder. "Besides, it would take a hell of a lot of shifters to take just *me* down, let alone the four of us."

Kavan stared at Beltine with wide eyes. He hadn't thought of that. His mate was a badass demon who could cast spells.

Feeling all his tension ease, Kavan relaxed. "Right."

"Here we are," Austin announced needlessly, parking the vehicle in front of a large house. "Let's go introduce ourselves."

"Indeed." Dane pushed open his door and slipped out. A second later, he opened Kavan's door. "Shall we go say hello?"

Seeing the teasing light in Dane's brown eyes as well as his jovial grin, Kavan couldn't help but chuckle. "I suppose."

Kavan exited the SUV, and Beltine fell into step beside him. Austin led with Dane flanking him, which surprised Kavan, but he would never presume to question Council Enforcer dynamics. As they climbed the stairs a few seconds later, it hit Kavan.

Austin led so he could be the first line of defense for Dane, if need be, who was actually in charge of their mission. The huge water buffalo shifter knocked firmly on the door. Then they waited . . . and waited.

After knocking again, Austin turned his head and arched a brow in silent question.

Dane pulled out his phone and woke the device. "Huh. It's already almost ten-thirty. Where does he work?"

"He's the town mayor," Kavan admitted.

Rolling his eyes, Dane muttered, "Of course, he is."

As they turned and headed back down the stairs, the crunch of tires on gravel drew their attention to a police car heading toward them.

"And the town sheriff and deputies are all probably shifters, too?" Austin guessed.

"Yes, sir."

Austin patted Kavan on the shoulder. "No need to be so formal in private. Just in public with these yahoos. Do you know who that is?"

Kavan knew Austin referred to the tall, muscular male climbing out from behind the wheel. "Head Enforcer Godfrey."

"All right." Austin lengthened his stride and took point again. "Enforcer Godfrey?" He continued without waiting for a response. "I'm Council Enforcer Austin O'Malley. This is Council Enforcer Dane Drudeson. We're here to escort Kavan to see his parents." When Austin indicated Kavan, Godfrey's eyes widened in obvious surprise. Austin didn't address it, continuing, "We intended to present ourselves to the alpha, as is customary, but we must have missed him before he headed to work."

"Holy fucking gods," Godfrey murmured, evidently finding his tongue. "Kavan? What are you doing back here? I thought you ran off with some guy and were never coming back." Rubbing the back of his neck, Godfrey admitted, "I don't think Alpha is gonna let you back in the territory, but you're well within your rights to visit your parents for a few days before moving on."

Kavan clenched his teeth, biting back a retort. After all, this male was the herd's head enforcer.

Beltine had no such problem. Growling under his breath, he stepped forward and declared, "Kavan didn't run away, with a guy or otherwise. He was kidnapped and held by witches for the last twelve years." Pointing his index finger at

Godfrey, he added, "And your alpha spreading lies meant no one knew to look for him. On behalf of my mate, I'm demanding restitution for his crimes."

Sucking in a sharp breath, Kavan stared at Beltine. "You're what?" he gasped.

"Now, wait just a minute," Godfrey responded gruffly. "Mate or not, you can't just come in here and demand restitution without any proof." He squinted at Beltine even as his neck started to flush. "Who are you, anyway?"

"There *is* plenty of proof, Enforcer Godfrey," Dane cut in, lifting a hand in placation. "As a council enforcer, I can carry out Beltine's wishes. I think it would be best if you escorted us to Alpha Anthony."

Enforcer Godfrey frowned at Beltine for a few more seconds before glancing between the two enforcers. Then he nodded. "Okay. Follow me." Then Godfrey returned to his cruiser.

As Kavan climbed into the SUV once more, he noticed Godfrey was already on the phone.

By the time they reached city hall, the entire inner circle was waiting for them. Sheriff Lancaster, the second, leaned against the staircase railing with his arms crossed. The second and third enforcers were there, too, one resting his butt on his cruiser hood while the second leaned against his truck.

"Well, if it isn't our wayward fag comin' home and causin' trouble," Sheriff Lancaster commented snidely. "You woulda been better off stayin' gone." Then Lancaster opened the door and pointed. "Well, come on in so we can get this bullshit story over with."

"Friendly fellow," Dane muttered as Austin led the way.

Nerves skittered up Kavan's spine as the three enforcers followed them inside.

"Makes me wonder," Beltine commented loudly, clearly not censoring his words. "If you all are here with us, who's patrolling the streets?"

"Never you mind about that," a shifter Kavan remembered as Rolston stated.

Kavan wondered when Rolston had been promoted to an enforcer position. He was a jerk at the best of times and a bully at the worst.

Damn, the herd has gone downhill since I was captured. Gonna definitely get my parents out of here.

"Get 'em in here, Beta," a booming voice that Kavan remembered well called from deeper in the building.

Soon, they all stood in a large conference room, where Alpha Anthony sat at the head. With his fingers steepled, he peered imperiously at Kavan. "Hello, Kavan. Back to cause trouble, I see. You should have stayed missing."

Godfrey glanced around. "Wait. I thought he'd run away."

Alpha Anthony lifted a hand, and Godfrey snapped his mouth shut.

"Looks like your alpha lied to you, Enforcer Godfrey," Beltine stated bluntly. He arched a brow as he peered at the alpha. "Let me guess. No cameras in here?"

A cold smile curved Anthony's face. "Nope. No cameras, so no one will be able to contest your claims that we *forced* you to change your mind about that restitution charge." Anthony snapped his fingers, and the sheriff started forward, as did the two deputies with him.

Godfrey looked on in confusion, clearly out of the loop.

"Well, I didn't want to kick your ex-alpha's ass, my *amina*," Beltine began with a shrug. "But it looks like I'm going to have to anyway."

As Beltine finished speaking, he must have dropped his glamour, for gasps filled the room. Their attackers froze as Anthony leaped to his feet.

"What the hell are you?" Anthony hollered.

Sheriff Lancaster seemed to regain his bravado, for he started forward again. The two deputies weren't so quick to back him up.

Austin crossed his arms over his massive torso and growled. "Un-fucking-believable." He exchanged a look with Dane, who grinned widely. Austin rolled his eyes.

"Alpha Anthony Sinclair, you are being taken into custody by the Shifter Council," Dane declared, grinning widely. "Your crimes are coordinating an attack on Shifter Council representatives as well as those under their charge."

Roaring in outrage, Anthony attacked. After a glance between them, the two deputies did, too. The sheriff lunged at Dane, while Godfrey lifted his hands in placation and took a step backward, clearly the smartest of the bunch.

Kavan watched in shock as Beltine quickly wiped the floor with the pair of deputies. A jab, a kick, and a swipe with a wing later, and both men were on the floor unconscious.

The sheriff didn't do any better with Dane. The big enforcer stepped to the side and swept out a leg, taking Lancaster's feet out from under him. The sheriff cartwheeled forward before slamming his head into the table. Dane grabbed the back of his shirt, hauled him up, only to slam his head into the table again—filling the room with an ominous crack. Then Dane released him, and Lancaster dropped like a brick.

Austin didn't even allow Anthony to get in a punch. When the alpha rushed him, he simply lifted a hand, his thumb and forefingers spread, and jabbed him in the throat. Anthony gasped as he stumbled backward, his eyes bugging out comically.

Grabbing Anthony's hair, Austin yanked downward as he brought his knee up. The crunch of the alpha's nose filled the room, followed by the shifter's scream. Shoving Anthony backward, Austin released him, allowing him to fall unceremoniously to the floor.

His lips pressed in a disdainful look, Austin stared at Anthony as he brushed his hands together as if clapping and wiping away something dirty.

Dane grinned broadly as he turned to Godfrey. "All right, Godfrey. You seem to have a bit of smarts or two." He pointed at the clearly shocked head enforcer. "Congratulations. You are interim alpha while the council gets all this shit sorted."

"I-I, uh, yes, Enforcer Dane," Godfrey stuttered, and Kavan thought that was the first time he'd ever seen the enforcer at a loss for words.

"Now then." Dane turned and faced Kavan. "Shall we go see your parents while Austin phones this in? I'm certain they'd love to see you."

Unable to help himself, Kavan asked, "Is Austin going to be safe alone here?"

Dane laughed. "Oh, yeah. He'll be grand."

Austin grinned for the first time since Kavan had met him. "Don't worry, buddy. I got this." Then he pulled out his phone as he began eyeing the shifters on the floor as if they were bugs that needed to be squashed.

"O-Okay then." Excitement flooded Kavan. "Yes, please."

After taking one step toward the door, Dane froze as he watched Beltine sling an arm around Kavan's waist. He pointed at the demon. "It's freaky how you can change your appearance right before my eyes."

Beltine laughed as he guided Kavan toward the door.

Evidently, his demon had put his glamour back in place.

Chapter Eleven

"Are you doing okay?" Beltine skimmed his palm up and down Kavan's side before helping him remove his shirt. "You're thinking awfully hard over there."

Sighing deeply, Kavan smiled at him over his shoulder. "Yeah . . ." he murmured, drawing out the word. Meeting his gaze, he admitted, "It was truly everything I'd hoped it could be."

Beltine pecked a kiss to Kavan's neck. "Your parents were thrilled to see you."

Having never had parents, Beltine didn't understand those sorts of ties. Still, he was happy for his *amina*. When Kavan's mother had seen him and started crying, he'd at first been worried. Then Beltine had realized they were tears of joy — also something he had no experience with.

"Yeah, they were." Kavan turned and twined his arms around Beltine's neck. "Thank you for being at my side. I'm not certain I could have done that without you."

"You could have," Beltine countered, rubbing up and down his spine, enjoying the feel of his *amina*'s warm flesh. "I have every faith in that." Dipping his head, Beltine nipped at Kavan's neck. "We can go see them anytime you want."

Kavan nodded before tightening his hold. "Thank you." His expression turned hungry. "But I really don't want to talk about them right now."

Feeling Kavan press his body flush to Beltine's own, he hummed appreciatively as he bucked his hips lightly. "Really?" Whispering into Kavan's ear, he asked huskily, "What could you possibly want to talk about?"

As Beltine spoke, he lowered one hand to Kavan's shorts-covered ass, wishing he were touching flesh. He pulled his *amina* as close as humanly possible while rocking his hips. His sexy shifter moaned wantonly, the sound so very sexy to Beltine.

"I can't wait until we're bonded tomorrow," Kavan mumbled breathily, rutting against him. "Feeling you is always so glorious, and I want you to be mine for eternity."

Beltine stilled, and he lifted his head. "It will hurt you."

Kavan smiled sweetly at him. "I know. I don't care."

Reading the sincerity, the certainty, in Kavan's deep hazel eyes, Beltine prayed to whatever gods cared to listen that his gorgeous *amina* wouldn't regret it later. He made a decision. "Let me give you a memory of what I wish I could be doing to you that you can think on while you're in pain tomorrow." Beltine gripped Kavan's ass, lifted, and tossed his shifter onto his nearby nest of pillows.

Barking a laugh, Kavan spread his arms and stared up at him. "I don't need a memory, however" — he spread his legs and lifted his arms over his head, stretching provocatively — "if you feel the need to ravish me, I won't complain."

Growling softly, Beltine grabbed his own fly and quickly undid it. He couldn't tear his gaze away from his shifter's long, lean lines as he pushed down his leather pants. Even hearing the pop of stitches couldn't get Beltine to tear his gaze away from the gorgeous sight before him.

"Come to bed, Beltine," Kavan urged, lifting a hand to him.

Beltine was all for that . . . except, he wanted to blow Kavan's mind, too. He *needed* to . . . needed to know that his shifter would remember how much he wanted to please him. With that thought in mind, Beltine eased onto the bed slowly and reached for his *amina*'s fly.

Hooking his clawed fingers into the waistband, Beltine

gave Kavan a wicked grin. Then he carefully swiped. He caught his sharp nails along a seam and rent the fabric off of his shifter's body from hip to thigh. Lifting his hands, Beltine took the fabric with it, baring Kavan's body to his gaze.

Kavan barked a laugh before saying, "I would have liked to wear those again."

"I'll get you more," Beltine promised, liking the smile on Kavan's face so much more than the formless cargo shorts. With a wink, he added, "Ones that showcase your ass."

Rolling onto his stomach, Kavan hiked his knees under him and arched his back, showing off said ass. "Like my ass, do you?" he teased, peering over his shoulder at Beltine. Hunger lit his hazel eyes. "Prove it."

Beltine's arousal flared, and his cock throbbed. Crawling into his nest of pillows behind Kavan, he grabbed his lover's thighs. "And how should I prove it?" he rumbled as he slid his palms up to grip Kavan's ass cheeks. "How about like this?"

Bending down, Beltine stuck out his tongue as he pulled Kavan's cheeks apart. He swiped his tongue over his *amina*'s wrinkled ring. His lover's musky taste exploded over his taste buds, lighting them up. With his mouth watering, Beltine pressed his face against Kavan's opening and thrust his tongue inside him.

Kavan howled beautifully and arched, and Beltine took complete advantage. Licking and lapping, he mapped every inch of his channel that he could reach. His lover's musky taste pleased his senses, and he couldn't resist searching for more.

"Oh, fuck, fuck, fuck, fuck," Kavan whined, shuddering and shivering in his grip. "Bels! Close!"

For an instant, Beltine lifted his face just enough and for long enough to say, "Do it." Then he dove back in, eating his *amina*'s ass for all he was worth . . . and it was a delicious ass.

"Beltine!"

Hearing Kavan scream his name enflamed the fire already thrumming through his veins. His cock throbbed between his thighs, and his balls tightened, forcing pre-cum to ooze from him. Need and desire surged through him, and he lunged upward.

Beltine draped himself over Kavan's trembling body. The smell of his lover's release perfumed the air, and he licked his lips in anticipation. Reaching between them, Beltine gripped the base of his cock and positioned it at Kavan's opening. Letting out a slow, deep breath, he waited as he smeared his fluid all over his lover's muscle.

"Yesss," Kavan slurred sluggishly. "Do it. Take me."

Rubbing his cheek over the back of Kavan's neck, Beltine applied a bit of pressure to his *amina*'s ring. He felt it begin to give, and a fresh wave of need ripped through his body. His balls reacted, pumping another dollop of pre-cum up his stalk.

"Soon," Beltine mumbled, doing his best to be patient. "I should have prepped you, but you tasted too damn good. Give my pre-cum a chance to do its work."

Kavan turned his head at that. His eyes were widely dilated, but there was still a question within their depths. "Huh?" he asked, ever-so-eloquently.

Beltine licked a line up Kavan's neck to his ear and suckled for an instant. When he felt the ring against his cock head soften and give, he heaved a sigh of relief. Beltine released Kavan's earlobe and began pushing forward.

"My pre-cum," Beltine rumbled, gritting his teeth as his *amina*'s channel opened and swallowed his knob in heat and pressure. "It causes your chute muscles to loosen, to soften and accept me into you." After another nip on Kavan's lobe, Beltine began slowly sliding deeper into his shifter's body as he added, "It also heightens your sensitivity."

Bottoming out, Beltine paused, a shudder working through him. "Gods, you're so tight." He licked over his claiming scar. "So perfect." Next, Beltine nipped his mark. "And all mine."

"Yesssss," Kavan hissed, rocking his body and pushing against him. "All yours." Turning his head, he awkwardly nipped at Beltine's chin. "And you're mine."

"I am," Beltine agreed wholeheartedly. "Now and forever."

Then, unable to hold still a second later, Beltine began to rut. He eased out slowly until Kavan's ring tugged against his flared crown. Moaning at the delicious sensation, he surged forward, driving into his *amina*.

Kavan's tight passage lit up the nerve endings all along Beltine's shaft. He pulled out, pushed in, only to pull out again. Over and over, Beltine slammed into his shifter's welcoming body.

To Beltine's delight, Kavan moaned and arched. He shivered and shuddered beneath him. Gripping the blanket, he even shoved back, meeting him in counterpoint to each rut.

"Mine," Beltine snarled, loving every second of coming together with his *amina*. "Ready to come again?"

Groaning, Kavan still managed to nod.

"Do it," Beltine urged right before he sank his teeth into his mark. At the same time, he thrust deep, driving as deeply into Kavan as he could go.

The heat of Kavan's body combined with the delicious flavor of his *amina*'s blood. Holding his shifter tight, Beltine felt his lover shudder in his grip. He clutched him close, reveling in the sensation of his shifter losing himself to pleasure. The scent of Kavan's seed perfuming the air was the final straw.

Beltine lost control, his orgasm coursing through him. His balls pulled tight, pumping his cum into his *amina*, marking his insides. He eased his teeth from Kavan's neck and roared his pleasure, ecstasy flowing through his body.

Feeling his *lackchet* ease from his piss-slit, Beltine trembled in anticipation. He anchored to Kavan, and his shifter's gasp and shudder tugged on his sensitive appendage. Micro-bursts of bliss rocked through Beltine's system, and he pumped more and more cum into Kavan's hot, willing body.

Floating on clouds of endorphins, Beltine clutched his *amina* tight. He eased them sideways, keeping them tucked close. Each shiver Kavan made caused an answering pulse of pleasure to course through Beltine.

Relaxing in his nest of pillows, Beltine cuddled around Kavan. He rubbed up and down his torso with one hand, while keeping his other arm tight around him. Sighing, he licked Kavan's still-bleeding bite mark, closing it.

Beltine knew that, due to Kavan's shifter healing, it would scar anew with an hour.

So sexy.

"Holy shit," Kavan mumbled, sighing deeply. Turning his head, he smiled almost drunkenly at Beltine. "That's so fucking fantastic. Is it always going to be like that?"

Grinning with satisfaction, Beltine admired the sated expression on Kavan's features. "If I'm doing it right, it will," he replied softly, nuzzling his nose over what he knew was sensitive skin behind his shifter's ear. Whispering huskily, Beltine promised, "And I will always endeavor to do it right."

CHAPTER TWELVE

"Just because we're standing around here monitoring things," Hank stated primly, clipping the edge of the sheer sheet to the tree. "It doesn't mean we have to be *watching* watching." Pointing at the other end of the blanket, he ordered, "Chissom, hang that up."

Chissom lifted his hands in placation, then did as he'd been told. Picking up his corner of the blanket, the vampire stretched it out and used a large clip to attach it to a nearby tree.

Hank grabbed another blanket he'd brought and ordered Knossis to help him with it.

Kavan turned away from the odd sight of a former blood donor offering privacy to the participants of a ritual bonding.

So very weird.

As Kavan watched Famine speak with his brothers, he stared in wonder. He couldn't believe that he was in the presence of the Four Horsemen of the Apocalypse, let alone the fact that they were about to combine their abilities in order to help Beltine bond with him early.

Evidently, just a few short years ago, this wouldn't have been possible. The brothers weren't always on the best of relations, and not that long ago, they were experiencing infighting. They often succumbed to pride, wanting to be the best — to have the most demons and to have the most generals.

Regardless of the *why*, Kavan appreciated that their behavior had changed and they were currently on good terms.

Demons Kavan didn't know milled around the forested

area, and he decided that sticking close to Hank wasn't such a bad idea. While Famine and Pestilence's demons were similar — pale, tall, and toned — War and Death's demons were entirely different. Those brothers' demons seemed to be built for battle — tall, black, thickly built, and heavily muscled.

Kavan supposed each had their pros and cons.

"Hey, my *amina*." Beltine slipped his arms around Kavan's waist, slotting up behind him. "You ready for this?"

Tipping his head, Kavan murmured, "Most definitely. I can't wait to be bound to you."

Even though Kavan had bitten Beltine, claimed him, he knew there was something missing. His animal did, too. He was in a near-constant state of arousal, his nature urging him to finish what they'd started.

Kavan couldn't imagine dealing with this unsettled sensation for decades.

Beltine urged Kavan to turn in his arms, then began to slowly peck kiss after kiss along his jawline. When his demon reached his ear, he suckled Kavan's earlobe, and a riot of warm tingles trickled down his torso. His nipples beaded, and goose bumps broke out over his arms.

"Oh, yes," Kavan murmured, loving every second of Beltine's sensual kisses. "Amazing."

"Okay, you love birds," Chissom called, interrupting their moment. He clapped his hands and grinned, showing off his fangs. "Let's get you into the center of the circle so we can get this party started."

As Beltine nodded, Kavan glanced around. There had to have been over a hundred demons milling around. The horsemens' chosen lovers were there, too, although Kavan couldn't remember who was whom. He even spotted Master Dante and a few others from the coven.

Taking a deep breath, Kavan followed Beltine, allowing his lover to tug him into the circle. The space was around twenty feet in diameter with lit candles creating the circumference. Hank's gauzy blankets were hung around five feet beyond the circle, creating a sheer curtain.

Considering the new moon intensifying the darkness and the candles contrasting it, Kavan imagined their silhouettes would be perfectly visible . . . hiding nothing.

Oh, well. It's the thought that counts.

"Come here, Kavan," Beltine urged, gripping the hem of his shirt. "Time to undress."

Nodding, Kavan lifted his arms. His demon had explained that they needed to be naked within the circle. Bending at the waist a bit, Kavan allowed Beltine to tug him free of his shirt.

With a wink, Beltine cast the item carelessly out of the circle.

Kavan chuckled nervously, but he began stripping the rest of his clothes himself. While toeing off his shoes, he unbuttoned his shorts. He paused for an instant before shoving them down and kicking them off. As Kavan bent and pulled off his socks, he tried not to feel self-conscious.

Shifters weren't shy about nudity in general. However, there were many, *many* people around who were *not* shifters. Getting naked had nothing to do with preparing to turn into his animal.

Picking up his clothes and shoes, Kavan carried it to the edge of the circle where Beltine had thrown his shirt. He did his best to not feel self-conscious, but it was tough. Then Kavan turned . . . and his breath caught in his throat.

Beltine stood at the center of the circle waiting for him. His strong, muscular demon stood tall and relaxed. He already had one hand wrapped around his jutting cock, stroking himself leisurely.

Kavan noticed the bead of pre-cum oozing from Beltine's wide slit. His mouth watered, and he vowed to eventually learn what the demon tasted like. In the past, he'd always been too busy succumbing to Beltine's expert love-making. Kavan would feel jealous, but he knew that he would be the recipient of those strokes and touches for the rest of their days.

"Kavan." Beltine lifted his hand, palm up. "Come to me."

Yanking his focus from Beltine's enticing groin, Kavan crossed to him and took his hand.

Smiling, Beltine lifted his hand and kissed his palm. He released his dick and wrapped his fingers around Kavan's nape instead. When Beltine tugged lightly, Kavan went with the move, accepting his demon's kiss.

Just like every time Beltine kissed him, Kavan soon lost himself in the sensuous slide of his lover's lips. He rested his palms on his demon's chest, feeling the strong muscles beneath the smooth skin. Sliding his hands upward, Kavan wrapped his arms around Beltine, pressing his naked body against the other male's.

In the next instant, Beltine wrapped an arm around Kavan's waist, and he felt himself spin. In his mind, he thought he should have slammed into the ground, but his talented demon laid him gently on the grass. Feeling Beltine's knee against his thighs, Kavan spread for his lover, welcoming him.

All the while, Beltine continued to plunder his mouth. He lapped at his tongue, teased at his gums, and plunged deep to taste his tonsils. Welcoming it all, Kavan dug his nails into Beltine's back and held on for the ride.

Kavan felt Beltine's cock touch his hole just as his mate ended the kiss on a gasp. Panting, Kavan slid his hands up Beltine's neck and threaded them into his demon's thick, white-blond locks. He shivered as he felt Beltine's pre-cum do its work, loosening his guardian muscles without a touch while increasing his sensitivity.

Groaning, Kavan lifted one leg and wrapped it around Beltine's waist. He tugged his mate closer, desperate for penetration, to feel his lover breach him. Kavan wanted to feel his demon stroke him from the inside out, sending him soaring to heights that he knew only his demon could achieve.

"Now," Kavan pleaded, holding Beltine's gaze. "Take me now."

"My *amina*," Beltine growled before sealing his mouth to Kavan's again.

Then Beltine plunged his shaft into Kavan, sinking deep, *deep* into his body.

Pushing out, Kavan welcomed his lover's taking.

Beltine immediately started a swift thrust and retreat, stabbing into his body over and over. Rocking his hips, Kavan welcomed each of his mate's ruts. He dug his fingernails into his demon's shoulders, hanging on as his senses lit up from the inside out.

Turning his head, Kavan broke the kiss only to call out Beltine's name.

"Yesss," Beltine snarled into his ear before demanding, "Offer me your soul."

Kavan struggled to gather enough air into his lungs, but he managed it. "Beltine, my mate, I offer you my soul."

The sound of a number of voices chanting filled the air around him. He recognized Famine's melodious tenor, and he guessed the others were his brothers. To his surprise, a deep red ring glowed all around them, and Kavan felt the hairs on his neck prickle.

Beltine gripped Kavan's jaw and urged him to focus on his intense gaze. "Come for me," he urged as he grabbed Kavan's dick and jacked it swiftly.

While Kavan gasped, his back bowed. His balls tightened, and his release crashed over him. As he flooded the space between them, his mind reeling on the release of endorphins, he vaguely noticed Beltine saying something in his native tongue.

Gonna have to learn that someday.

The thought passed in and out of Kavan's mind as Beltine leaned close to him once more. He thought his mate was going to kiss him, but he stopped just shy. With his lips hovering over Kavan's, Beltine whispered a few more words . . . then sucked.

A shard of pain stabbed through Kavan's chest. He gasped as it intensified, then let it out in an agonizing scream. His chest felt as if someone were trying to tear open his ribcage and reach inside it.

Kavan jolted and shuddered. His hands dug into the earth beneath him, and he tried to shimmy away from . . . whatever.

The slight sting of something in his rectum registered, giving him something else to focus on. He recognized Beltine's *lackchet* attached to his prostate, and he was finally able to suck in a surprised breath. Light shocks of pleasure began to trickle up his chest, causing the painful agony to ebb just a little . . . just enough for him to focus.

Kavan remembered where they were, what they were doing, and why. He reminded himself that the pain was fleeting, and in return, he would have a lifetime.

A fair trade.

Snapping his mouth shut, Kavan stopped the scream that he didn't even realize he'd been uttering. He lifted his hands from the grass, ignoring the fact that they were dirty. Kavan wrapped his arms around Beltine's muscular torso and embraced whatever change was happening to him, pain or not.

While Kavan's insides still felt like molten fire coursed within him, he no longer felt flayed by it. Instead, the heat in his torso signified something else to him—union. By undergoing the fire of change, Kavan would be able to keep his demon until the end of time.

Finally, the pain began to ebb, and not due to the continued stimulation of Beltine's *lackchet.*

Kavan finally managed to draw in a full breath, and he whispered Beltine's name. "Beltine . . . my mate." He tugged his demon's thick hair, using it to get his lover to lift his head. Spotting the regret in his demon's ice-blue eyes, Kavan smiled and touched his lips. "It's over. Kiss me."

Beltine's regret morphed into the sweetest look of relief and adoration. His demon gave in to his urgings and sealed his mouth over Kavan's own.

For the next several minutes, Kavan lost himself — again — in Beltine's kiss. He enjoyed his masculine flavor and the skill of his tongue. Sliding his palms over his demon's body, Kavan touched every inch of his flesh that he could reach.

When Beltine eased the kiss to an end, Kavan let him. He peered up at his mate and smiled, feeling tired but happy — complete in a way he hadn't realized he could.

"How are you feeling?" Beltine asked quietly, threading his fingers through Kavan's hair. "Okay now?"

Kavan nodded. "Yeah." His voice sounded a little scratchy, and he hoped he hadn't been screaming too long before he'd managed to control himself. "I'm okay." Then Kavan grinned. "Better than. For the first time in my life, I feel complete."

"Me, too," Beltine admitted. His brows furrowed as he admitted, "Although, you had me worried for a moment there."

"I'm sorry about that." Kavan knew he hadn't been able to help himself. It truly had been damn painful. "It's fine now, and we never have to do this again."

"Good thing, too!" a deep voice called from outside the circle. "Although you did miss all the fun."

Kavan cocked his head and mouthed *who?*

Beltine grimaced and replied softly, "War." Then his demon frowned. "What fun?" he called back.

That same voice replied. "The witches attacked." War snorted as he added, "Guess all Kavan's hollerin' drowned out the noise of battle."

"Leave them alone, War," a tenor male voice chastised. "That's not very nice."

Gaping, Kavan looked Beltine's way again.

"Xerxes," Beltine whispered, and Kavan knew that was War's small shifter mate.

Then War's words registered, and he groaned, throwing his arm over his face. "So embarrassing."

Beltine growled and grabbed his arm, forcing it up. Pinning Kavan with a hard glare, he stated, "You endured something no one else in the world has. You have nothing to be embarrassed about." Then Beltine's eyes narrowed. "And if anyone gives you shit about it, I'll shred them."

"None of us would do that." Kavan recognized that voice as Knossis. "Hell, I can't think of any of us who'd want to go through what you did. Kudos, man. Now enjoy your afterglow while we clean up this fucking mess."

Kavan bit back a laugh, grinning from ear to ear. He decided to do exactly as the dominant fox shifter had suggested. Grabbing Beltine's head, he drew his demon into a deep kiss.

After all, it would still be a while before his *lackchet* released, and Kavan planned to enjoy every damn second of it.

ABOUT THE AUTHOR

Charlie started writing fantasy when she was eight, and after stumbling onto her first erotic romance at age nineteen, she realized her true calling. She now focuses on writing gay erotic romance, normally of the paranormal variety, with heroes of all kinds. With the help and support of her husband, Charlie finally fulfilled one of her life-long goals . . . move to acreage with her horses. You can often find her curled up with her laptop and a cup of tea or glass of wine, creating her next adventure. Charlie enjoys exploring the mountains of her new Oregon home on horseback, 4-wheeler, or motorcycle.

She can be reached at ch.richards2010@yahoo.com
Or visit her at www.charlie-richards.com